Last Mile to Nogales

Nogales was a hell town like no other. A sun-stricken noplace in the heart of the desert, its single claim to fame was the band of deadly guns-for-hire who called it home and it was home for Ryan Coder, whom some saw as the gun king.

Yet, fast as he was, Coder found his life on the line when he was hired out to the king of Chad Valley, only to find himself pitted against Holly, the youngest and deadliest gunslinger of them all.

Would Coder find himself just another notch on Holly's gun?

The Immortal Marshal
Get Dellinger
Two for Sonora
One Last Notch
Lobo
In the Name of the Gun

Last Mile to Nogales

Ryan Bodie

A Black Horse Western

ROBERT HALE · LONDON

© Ryan Bodie 2008
First published in Great Britain 2008

ISBN 978-0-7090-8609-3

Robert Hale Limited
Clerkenwell House
Clerkenwell Green
London EC1R 0HT

www.halebooks.com

Typeset by
Derek Doyle & Associates, Shaw Heath
Printed and bound in Great Britain by
CPI Antony Rowe, Wiltshire

CHAPTER 1

GUN JOB

'Just how good are you with that gun, Shilleen?'

'Good enough.'

'Good enough to kill Wardlaw?'

'Sure.'

'Then you're hired.'

'We ain't talked money yet.'

'I hear you work cheap.'

'You heard wrong then.'

'All right, how much?'

'A hundred now, a hundred when he's dead.'

'You've got a deal. Here's your first hundred. When will you do it?'

'Tonight.'

'Where?'

'Up at the big house.'

'He's well guarded up there.'

'Them Regulators? Pah! They won't stop me.'

'They'd better not. But if they did, don't blab who hired you.'

'How could I do that? I don't even know your name, only that you're with the miners.'

'And that's all you need to know. Do it and meet me back here tomorrow night, same time. I'll have the other hundred and maybe a bonus if you do the job right.'

'Pleasure doing business with you, mister.'

'Good night.'

'Good night – boss.'

Foley Wardlaw looked up sharply as his wife swept into their chandeliered dining room.

'Well, about time you came down. I've been waiting half an hour.'

'What a gracious greeting, darling,' the woman replied as she pirouetted before him. 'How do you like my new gown?'

'How the hell much did that cost me?'

Rhea Wardlaw turned her back and ignored the question as she admired her glittering image in the floor-length wall mirror. Taller than average and built on the long slender lines of a thoroughbred, she was a picture of glamor sheathed in a clinging creation of finest blue silk with long silver rings dangling from delicately shaped ears.

She smiled the cold, knowing smile of a woman sure of her power when she saw Wardlaw's expression change from anger to desire in the glimmering mirror.

'My chair, Foley,' she said, turning back to the table.

'Damnit, we're not back in Boston now, Rhea,' he protested. 'And I'm not one of your slippery Eastern heel-clickers, either.'

'My chair, Foley!'

Wardlaw didn't rise right away. The mining magnate known throughout Wyoming as the king of Chad Valley wasn't used to being ordered about by anybody. Tall and iron-featured at fifty with steel-grey hair and a rat-trap mouth, Wardlaw was accustomed to having people draw out chairs for him, not the other way round.

His annoyance only survived for as long as it took for his attention to return to his wife, when pride and resolve deserted him completely. Cursing the weakness that ran through him at such times he rose and submissively held the chair out for her while she seated herself fussily, elaborately arranging her skirt.

He kissed her bare shoulder. She flinched.

'Really, Foley, don't you think it's too hot for that sort of thing?'

'Hot?' Wardlaw snapped, testy again in an instant. He moved to his straight-backed chair and sat down hard. 'I don't believe it's the heat we have to worry about in this house, Rhea, rather the opposite. Every time I go near you lately you seem to freeze up like a—'

'Please, darling, I'm in no mood either for your

colorful imagery or for your tiresome complaints regarding my capacity as a lover.'

Wardlaw flushed darkly.

'By God, Rhea, sometimes you talk just like a whore – damned if you don't!'

'I'll have turtle.'

Wardlaw gaped, swore. 'What?' he said. Then he realized the Mexican houseboy had entered, silently as always. His wife was ordering soup.

'By Judas, one day I'll have your liver for creeping up on me like that, boy!' he snarled, focusing his anger on a less formidable target.

'Oh, let the man be, Foley,' Rhea said boredly. 'You can't blame the servants just because you're all jittery and terrified somebody is going to try to murder you.'

'You don't give a damn, do you?' he retorted. 'You don't care a toss that both my mines are idle right now. Or that those ignorant sons of Irish layabouts won't agree to go back underground until I spend thousands on new shoring timbers. You couldn't care less that there's been one attempt upon my life already and—'

'We'll both have the turtle soup,' Rhea cut in, smiling at José. 'And what will you have for the main course – darling?'

Wardlaw sometimes feared he might lose his temper completely at moments like this and maybe do something really crazy. But as always he only had to drink in her lithe feline beauty and wait for lust to kick in for him to achieve something like calm.

'Veal!' he almost shouted and the servant whispered from sight.

A thick silence fell with Rhea turning her head from side to side to admire her reflection in the big windows overlooking the sweeping emerald lawns, the hot and dusty town sprawled far below. Wardlaw studied her from beneath glowering brows, desire and anger battling for supremacy in his face.

In the prolonged silence both clearly heard the sounds of a horse drawing up outside. Wardlaw turned his head sharply.

'That must be Slater.'

'Well, if it is he can wait until after we've dined.'

'No, he can't.' Wardlaw raised his voice. 'That you, Slater?'

'Yeah, boss.'

'Well, get in here, damnit!'

Slater pushed open the door. He was accompanied by Neeley, Wardlaw's dapper Mines Manager.

'Honestly, Foley,' Rhea admonished, 'there's no reason why this can't wait. Your precious mines aren't going to cave in during the next half-hour, are they?'

The tall man looked aggrieved.

'I'm not worried about the goddamn mines,' he snapped. 'I've had Slater checking on that rumor the miners are plotting to hire somebody to kill me.'

His wife stifled a yawn and gazed at the ceiling.

Slater began, hat in his hands. 'Evening, boss – ma'am.'

'Well?' Wardlaw snapped.

Runty and ugly, the gunman glanced uncertainly at Rhea, who ignored him.

'You can speak freely before my wife, man,' Wardlaw said. 'Mrs Wardlaw chooses not to believe my life is in any danger.'

'You don't, ma'am?' Slater said. 'By the tarnal, I wouldn't be too sure about that—'

'You have crumbs in your whiskers, Mr Slater,' the woman said.

The man reddened and brushed at his short dark beard. A tough and dangerous man of the gun, Slater felt and often acted like a schoolboy when in the presence of the boss's wife.

Red-faced now, he turned back to Wardlaw.

'There's still rumors floating about, boss. But nothing solid to go on.'

'Any new faces in town?'

'Well, there's always somebody or other drifting through.'

'Anyone special today?'

Slater shrugged. 'I see Deagan's got a new man dealing faro.'

Wardlaw's eyes narrowed at mention of that name. He was deeply suspicious of the only other man who even remotely challenged his power in Chad Valley, the big-time gambler and saloon-keeper Ace Deagan.

'Anything else?' he growled.

Slater nodded. 'Those two hardcases who drifted in yesterday, Brogan and Shilleen. They're still about

10

. . . not sure just who or what they are yet.'

Wardlaw scowled, reflecting upon the many problems which always seemed to be accumulating and demanding his attention.

He remembered suddenly that he'd wired the Wyoming Mining Company in Durango regarding the possibility of their supplying strike-breakers in order to get his mines operating again.

'What'd the company say?' he wanted to know, turning to Neeley.

'They can't help us right now,' the Mines Manager said.

Wardlaw cursed.

'I knew I couldn't rely on those ingrates.' He gestured. 'All right, Neeley, go wire Mid-Western in Cheyenne.'

Neeley stepped past Rhea's chair on his way out, tried to catch the woman's eye but failed. Unaware, Wardlaw swallowed some soup then scowled.

'Well, get busy,' he ordered. 'But keep sharp, I smell something in the air tonight, damnit!'

Slater and Neeley left and the entrée arrived. Husband and wife bickered their way through the course as they did the veal cooked in red wine, the peach ice-cream and the brandy.

It seemed the woman won each verbal encounter on this occasion yet for once this didn't really bother Wardlaw. It was genuinely serious business that dominated his thoughts tonight.

The ongoing stubbornness and tenacity of his

striking miners puzzled the tycoon. Seven long weeks without a dollar between them in pay, their kids going hungry and their women growing more desperate by the day – yet they still refused to cave in and return to work. What kept the idiots going?

'Foley.'

'What?'

'About my vacation—'

That was as far as his wife got when from outside came the roar of a gun and a window went out with a crash as something small and lethal whistled over Wardlaw's head.

'Down!' he roared and the couple dived beneath the table as a second gunblast sounded. The shot was still echoing as the crouching couple grew aware of raised voices, hoarse shouts and the sounds of a struggle from the gardens. Moments later Slater's voice sounded from the darkness.

'We got the varmint, boss!'

Wardlaw was on his feet in an instant. 'You stay put!' he shouted to Rhea, who showed no inclination to move, then rushed out into the night.

He immediately sighted figures struggling over by the rose arbor. Approaching warily he realized Slater and two Regulators had hold of a hatchet-faced stranger with blood running from his mouth. As Wardlaw came up Slater ripped his elbow into the man's guts, causing him to jacknife and puke.

'Who the hell is he?' Wardlaw panted.

'Shilleen,' Slater panted. 'One of them gunslicks

12

that's been hanging around recent.' He smacked the captive violently across the back of the head causing him to nosedive into the dirt. Slater jammed a big boot on his neck and held him pinned, a man who always played the game hard. 'He must've sneaked in mighty sly, boss.'

Wardlaw was slowly recovering by this. 'Who hired you?' he demanded.

'Go straight to hell!' gasped the gun for hire.

Wardlaw snapped his fingers. Robards passed him his bowie knife. The mines boss was over his scare, cold rage replacing it now. He jabbed the prone figure in the ribs and the crimson flowed.

'You stinking—' Shilleen began, but the haft of the bowie crashed into his mouth, silencing him as he was hauled upright by strong hands. Wardlaw's eyes were crazy now. The mining tycoon had been under pressure for weeks on end and the realization he might well have been killed just now caused something inside him to snap.

His imagination conjured up a vivid image of himself and Rhea sprawled side by side upon their fine Persian carpet spilling crimson, just as this killer was now.

Without a moment's deliberation Wardlaw plunged the heavy knife to the hilt in the man's heart. Shocked, Slater, Robards and Miles jumped back as the body thudded to earth, dead even before it struck.

Unrepentant and exhilarated, the reaction of the richest man in town was almost frightening as he swung wildly upon Slater.

'That does it for you, Slater!' he panted. 'Only for luck this bastard would have killed me.'

'But, boss—'

'But nothing!' Wardlaw snarled, striding away to meet Neeley as the man came rushing out. He propped and jabbed Neeley in the chest. Hard.

'That's the very last time anybody will ever threaten my life, Neeley. I want you to go hire the best gunfighter in Wyoming – in the whole goddamned West if needs be. I don't give a hoot what he costs or what sort of a swine he might be, just so long as I can depend on him to do his job and protect me and what I own. Do you understand?'

'S-sure I do . . .' Neeley croaked dryly, squinting back at the dead man by the rose arbor.

'Then never mind standing there gaping like a fool. Get busy!'

'Yes, sir, Mr Wardlaw!'

CHAPTER 2

WHERE GUNHAWKS ROOST

Nogales, for all its wide notoriety, was not so much a town as merely an untidy scatter of unpainted plank constructions squatting out there upon the wide dun plains of the Crow River desert country in the middle of noplace.

Comprising smithy, hotel-cum-saloon, eatery, three tumbledown shacks and a rusted water tank, it was a dusty, ugly little hole fifty miles from the nearest town and a thousand miles from respectability.

Even the soft lavender dusk which stole in from across the Burning Plains that evening failed to invest the place with even a hint of primitive beauty.

The gloom deepened and one by one the lights went on to form a frail ring of life against the silent menace of the great flatlands beyond.

It was time for Tone-Deaf Tanner to take his first drink of the day, flex his unskilled fingers and prepare himself for the opening tune of the evening at the piano of the High Rider Saloon.

Over at his livery-cum-smithy, Flannigan was banging a horseshoe with a steel hammer and singing about his old mother whom he'd sent to an early grave with his wild and desperate ways before finding himself a refuge from the law out here where even the bravest lawmen never trod.

A gaunt yellow dog went sniffing along the street then sharply lifted its head, listening.

Far out upon the plains a single rider was coming in with the dark.

For a place as lonesome and notorious as Nogales the arrival of anybody was rarely a cause for either alarm or unease. There were men here who would be hanged on sight without trial in most places beyond the plains, but here all were safe. Nogales was too remote and deadly dangerous for the law, the Rangers or even the Army to threaten the dark lives that were lived out here.

Every now and again one of their number might fall foul of American justice someplace far from here, but never in Nogales itself. Here they were safe from virtually anybody except others of their own kind.

So it was that as the still unidentified horseman became dimly visible beyond the frail rim of the lights, nobody showed any signs of nervousness or unease. Plainly this had to be one of their own.

The rider finally clop-hoofed fully into the light and, seeing who it was, everybody just nodded and returned to the drinking and gambling.

For the new arrival was the man who more than any other had helped put Nogales on the Territory map over recent years.

He stepped down and mounted the weathered porch of the saloon to shoulder through the batwings.

He halted just inside and every head in the place turned his way. There were nods, murmured greetings, here and there a flicker of nervousness. His expression revealed nothing as his deep brown eyes flickered over Wyoming's fast gun elite. Then, fingering his hat back from his brow, Ryan Coder made his slow and deliberate way across to the low plank bar.

Where his tequila was already waiting.

'Good to see you back, Ryan,' grinned Coley Dent, back-shooter and kidnapper, and – ever since a U.S. Marshal had shot out one of his ugly eyes and his courage along with it – the saloon-keeper cum sage of the High Rider Saloon. He winked roguishly. 'Heard about you running a scare through them Whipple Creek Boys up north, heh, heh! Guess it'll be a long time afore those polecats feel like raising hell anyplace again, eh? Hey, hey!'

Coder went to a corner table and sampled his drink. Surrounded in the main by gaunt and lean-bodied men of the gun, this Nogales six-gunner was by contrast broad-shouldered and heavy set with a mane of black hair and powerful, strong-boned features.

This remote dot far out upon the bone-dry plains had been his base for five years and might continue being so until he either quit the game ... or the other thing.

'The other thing' was Nogales-speak for death by gunshot.

Although he considered himself as vulnerable as the next man, Coder never dwelt on the dangers of his profession. He was a gunfighter because he'd been born fast and this place was the closest thing to a real home he'd ever known. And with friends with names like Juarez, Jordan, Kip Ryan and Walker, these dangerous men were as close to kinfolk as he was ever likely to know.

Drinkers watched as he sampled his first shot. They were all of his own kind, cold-eyed shootists in the main, some young, some old, a few deeply morose and one or two even light-hearted and cheerful. This was the remote noplace the fast guns headed for to rest up between jobs or to meet up with their contacts. It was a fortress of fear where even the James Gang had felt obliged to tread warily upon passing through once with the Youngers on their way to Oregon a year before. For each of these men had, by right of guts and gunspeed, won a place in that gunfighter hierarchy of which Coder was likely the very top ranker.

18

He sprinkled salt on the back of his hand, licked it, downed his tequila, put a slice of lemon to his lips then gazed into the mirror behind the bar.

Several met his gaze in the glass including the man in the expensive suit seated alone in the far corner. The stranger had client written all over him.

'Who?' Coder asked. His voice was deep and resonant.

'Didn't say. Been here two days,' Dent supplied.

'That's a long time to wait.'

'That's what I figured.'

Coder's gaze roamed the gloomy room to focus upon the bunch gathered around the faro layout. The tall and flashy young man in the middle was Holly, one of the swiftest and deadliest men God ever put breath into.

'Has Holly been here all that time?' he asked quietly.

'Yeah.'

'So, howcome he's not showing any interest in the stranger? He smells of dollars to me.'

'Why not? On account that dude has been waiting for you to show, is why.'

Coder nodded understandingly. Holly would resent that, he knew. Lucky it didn't matter a plug damn to him what Holly liked or didn't.

The moment Coder started toward the stranger Holly stepped away from his group to block his path. As lean as a whip with a small reptilian head and bitter black eyes, the fair-headed shootist moved with a silky grace in his patent leather boots.

'Some of us boys want to talk to you, Coder.'

'What about?' Standing face-to-face the fast guns afforded a sharp contrast – Holly lithe and flashy, Coder soberly garbed and built like a blacksmith.

'That Big S job. We just been waiting for you to get back so's you could join us.'

'I don't recall saying I'd ride with you on that deal,' said Coder, still studying the man over in the corner, weighing him up with his eyes.

'We need you.'

Coder had already guessed that. The Big S spread across the border in Colorado was currently locked in a life or death struggle with the cowtown of Weed. It was the potentially messy kind of situation he liked to pass up whenever possible. He'd made that clear here before leaving on his last assignment, did so again now.

Holly's cold stare plunged to sub zero.

'I said we need you, Coder.'

'You're all out of luck in that case,' Coder murmured and, pushing past, crossed to the stranger in the corner and sat down.

'You're Coder?' The man was tall and expensively dressed. Under heavily pomaded hair, his face was nervous.

'I'm Coder. Who are you?'

'You really are Ryan Coder?'

Coder frowned. 'Why would I lie?'

'I don't know. Maybe it's just that I don't think you

really look like a gunfighter.'

A faint smile touched Coder's lips.

'That's been said before. Many times, in fact. Maybe you should ask some of these people here who I am?'

The stranger shook his head slowly.

'No . . . no, I don't believe that's necessary. Now I am looking at you up close I can see. . . .'

'See what?' Coder challenged. 'The dead men in my eyes?'

'No . . . no, I didn't mean that—'

'I was joking. So, let's get down to business. Who are you and what do you want?'

'My name's Coe Neeley. I'm Mines Manager for Mr Wardlaw of Sedalia. You've heard of him, perhaps?'

'In passing.' Coder took out a thin cigarillo and applied a match. 'There's big trouble with the miners up there, I hear tell?'

'Really big. They haven't worked in seven weeks. They are what the Easterners call "on strike".'

Coder leaned back, the chair creaking under his weight. 'I won't turn my gun against a working man.'

Neeley blinked. 'That's not what we had in mind. But why wouldn't you accept such a job if you were asked?'

'It's simply not a fair match – a gunslinger against workers. I'm too fast.'

For Neeley this declaration added weight to the strong impression the gunfighter had already created since entering. On this assignment, he'd expected to find himself dealing with some mean and cold-eyed killer, a description that scarcely fitted the man seated before him now.

He cleared his throat. 'Well, we won't go into that on account there's no need. Mr Wardlaw finds himself in need of a personal bodyguard, as he's living in fear of his life. Already there have been two attempts made to kill him.'

'And that's the job you want me to take on?'

'Yes.'

'All right.'

Neeley's brows went up. During his time spent waiting around this hell-hole for the gunfighter's return he'd been warned Coder might prove a tough haggler over terms, money and details. He'd not expected such ready acceptance.

'What about your fee?' he asked after a moment.

'I'll work that out with Wardlaw himself.' Coder rose. 'But you can relax, man. I've never turned down a man yet who came to me looking for simple protection. I'll go see about a fresh horse.'

With Neeley trailing, Coder headed for the batwings. He'd forgotten about Holly and the others. But they hadn't forgotten him, as he realized when all rose from their chairs at his aproach. He turned to confront them.

'Sorry, boys, but I can't make Colorado with you.'

There was a murmur of disappointment, and something more. Though these men respected Coder there was little genuine liking for him here due to the gunman's aloofness, often seen as arrogance. He never mixed with hired guns. He was a loner by nature and by choice.

This entrenched resentment was deepened by his rejection of their offer now, which offended the high-stepping Holly.

'You mean you've gone and took a job from an outsider after you knew we wanted you with us, Coder?' the man challenged, his face sheening in the light. 'I don't take to that at all kindly!'

Tone-Deaf Tanner's fingers came to an abrupt halt upon the piano keys. Coley Dent froze midway through pouring a beer for ever-dry California Jack Driscoll. In this place where a smart man chose his words more carefully than most anyplace else on the map, Holly's outburst seemed dangerously challenging.

Coder met glittering black eyes impassively. Holly was a true pro. One cardinal rule of survival here amongst the top guns was never to cross swords with anybody of your own calibre. That could prove one of the surest ways known for a man to reduce his life-expectancy in this deadly town.

'A man wants me to bodyguard him up Sedalia way,' Coder explained. 'To me that appeals more than shooting up women and kids in your war. In any case, you don't need me. There's already six of you ready to go – right?'

None of the bunch responded; they simply looked uneasy.

'Well?' Coder snapped. 'Is that so or ain't it?'

Buck Heller had ridden with Coder on several assignments. He cleared his throat. 'Afraid there's more, Ryan. You see, the Big S says it don't want us unless you're with us.'

Coder's stare cut back to Holly. Now he understood. Holly was put out because the big ranch had laid down that stipulation. The man's pride was hurt. Tough!

'That's not my fault,' he murmured and turned to leave.

'Hold it, Coder!'

'What?' His tone was sharp as he turned.

'This just ain't good enough, is what. I don't mind you sashaying around like you're God Almighty, like you do. But when you go out of your way to stop us getting a high-paying contract then I object plenty. I reckon maybe you ought to reconsider and go tell that hirer of yours you got a prior committment.'

'OK,' Coder said, allowing his gaze to flicker from one hard face to another. 'I'll do that.'

The gunfighters were taken aback. They'd never expected him to cave in so meekly. But the gunfighter was faking. He'd sensed Holly was geared up to force a showdown on this issue, and he meant to get in first. For a moment all were off guard and in that split-second Coder was lunging towards the gunman with right fist blurring.

Too late the lethal Holly saw his danger. He cursed and slashed at his hip. But Coder was too quick. His arm blurred and fist crashed against jawbone with a sound like a kicked cigar box. The gunfighter was belted backwards against the wall. He buckled at the knees and fell forwards to the floor, out cold.

A hatchet-faced side-kick reached for his gun. He froze on realizing a big black Colt .45 had appeared in Coder's right fist as if by sleight-of-hand.

'Go ahead and draw if you've a mind, Fulton,' Coder said. 'I've killed better men than you for less.'

Over behind his bar, runty Coley Dent slowly lowered himself out of sight . . . and there were a dozen others in the place who wished they could do the same. Ryan Coder with a naked Colt in his hand was a chilling sight to see.

There was an audible sigh of relief when that black .45 finally slipped back into leather.

'Holly's ambitious,' Coder stated. 'Too much so. He wants to wear my hat but he's not man enough to do that yet. He might never be. But maybe that smack in the head will shake his brain up a little. When he comes to, tell him I'd get shook of any ideas he might have of getting square. He'll live longer if he does.'

He paused a moment to let that sink in.

'I saw a couple of you thinking about backing his play just now. Well, remember this . . . and you can pass this on to Holly when he comes to. Next time anybody tries to bunch up on me I won't use my fists. You compre that, second-raters?'

It was tough talk but effective and with Coder

standing before them empty-handed and challenging, not a man blinked or moved as much as a finger.

The tableau held as Coder turned his wide back and stepped over Holly's still motionless form to make for the louvered doors. He snapped his fingers and a white-faced Coe Neeley managed to get his legs working and trailed him from the room.

Only when the batwings had swung to stillness behind him did the gunfighters of Nogales begin to breathe easier.

It was a long time since Coder had come down so hard here. They would remember it.

The sounds of the men's leaving had long since faded into the night before Holly was fully revived. He eventually got to his feet unaided, dabbing at a bloodied mouth. Dangerous men stepped back uneasily for he was as renowned for temper as for gunspeed.

But there was no outburst or rage, just an icy calm that seemed even more chilling.

'He's a dead man,' Holly breathed at length. 'You know that, don't you?'

Nobody answered. There was no need.

'But I'll bide my time.' The fast gun touched his lips, looked at the blood on his fingers. 'Then I'll kill him.'

He paused and his stare flicked from face to face. 'Anybody wanna claim I can't do it?'

No takers.

Satisfied, Holly sleeved his swollen mouth one last

time, tugged down the lapels of his fancy waistcoat and then nodded to Keller.

'OK, Buck, I could stand a shot.'

Coley Dent reached for his glasses. Tone-Deaf Tanner attacked the piano again, so shaken by events that for several bars he couldn't stay in tune. The killers drank as Coley Dent wiped his bar, and the wind blew stronger from the south.

CHAPTER 3

RHEA

'Mrs Wardlaw, you can't be getting around in the house in just that!'

Standing in the door of her upstairs bedroom, Rhea Wardlaw fanned herself with the latest copy of an Eastern fashion periodical and frowned at the maid.

'And why not?' she said, small droplets of perspiration on brow and cheek.

'Why – why I can see clear through it, is why.' Abigail rolled her eyes in disapproval. 'I swear you got nothing on under that there chemise.'

Rhea Wardlaw laughed throaty and low. The maid was one of the very few who escaped the caustic lash of her tongue here at the mansion. That elderly lady had been her maidservant back in Boston in her single years and had come West with her. She was easily shocked. Rhea herself had been shockable back in her single days, seemingly an eternity ago now even though it was in reality but two years. Two years with a man she both feared and no longer loved had taken care of that.

'Yes I have, Abby,' she said. 'Not that it matters much anyway. There's nobody around to see.'

'That's where you're wrong, ma'am. Mr Wardlaw and Mr Neeley is just downstairs with some fella I never seen before.'

Rhea frowned. She'd not heard anybody arrive. Then she realized she must have dozed before the heat forced her from the stifling drawing room. Barefooted, she crossed to the ornately worked redwood railing to look down into the large foyer. As she did, Coe Neeley emerged from Wardlaw's study, glanced up then started up the stairs.

'Go down and tend to the sheets, Abby,' she ordered.

'But, Mrs Wardlaw, that's Mr Neeley coming up, and you ain't got no more on than—'

'Oh, don't burst a blood vessel, Abby,' she sighed, making for her room. 'I'll put a housecoat over it – and sweat like a pig – just for you.'

The maid left, shaking her head and muttering. Rhea went to her wardrobe and began flicking listlessly through her clothes. At the sound of a step, she called, 'In here, Coe.'

Neeley entered. The man was travel-stained and red-eyed from the dust. His weariness appeared to vanish at sight of her. She stood silhouetted against the light coming through the windows. He came to her swiftly, hungrily. His arms went about her, pressing her fiercely against himself. For a moment she seemed to accept his embrace then thrust him away.

'You're getting reckless, Coe,' she said boredly, turning her back and fiddling with her wardrobe again. 'One day Mr Big will catch you doing something like that . . . and Mr Big will make you wish you'd never been born.'

Neeley's gaze played over her sensuous body which was tantalizingly visible through the flimsy material of her shift. He had to wet his lips with his tongue before he could speak.

'I don't give a damn, Rhea,' he said unevenly. 'I don't care if he does find out—'

'Oh, yes you do, Coe,' she said, turning back to him and smiling as she held a pretty cotton frock against her body. 'Be honest, for once. Foley terrifies you. If he were to walk through that door right now I wouldn't be a bit surprised to see you faint.'

The swift denial on Neeley's lips died stillborn and he jerked his head around in a sudden, jittery way to make doubly sure his employer was not standing there.

Rhea's throaty laugh filled the room.

'Oh, poor Coe. You do suffer so, don't you? But answer me seriously, darling – do you think this suits me or not?'

Anger tinged the man's cheeks, and he muttered a curse as he made to embrace her again.

'That's quite enough!' she snapped.

Confused and angry with his own weakness as much as her capriciousness, the man stepped back. 'Damnit, Rhea, I haven't seen you for more than a minute or two in all this time—'

'Were you finally able to get your gunfighter?' she cut in.

The remark was timely. It reminded Neeley of the real reason he'd come upstairs.

'Yes,' he said glumly. 'Wardlaw wants you to come down and meet him.'

She whirled sharply. 'You mean this . . . this person is already here? In my home?'

'Uh-huh. Showed up out of noplace about half an hour ago.'

'And just what on earth kind of a creature is he?' Her red-painted mouth twisted in disgust.

'Surprising. . . .'

'What sort of description is that? Oh, never mind. It doesn't matter. But why on earth would Foley want me to meet some dirty little killer or whatever species he might be? Surely Slater is bad enough. What charming habits does this one have? Is it housebroken?'

Neeley scratched the back of his neck. 'Well, to be truthful . . . he's not much like the other guntippers. . . .'

'Pshaw! They're all alike. And I detest and despise every single one of them, what with their boasting and their strutting and always playing with their weapons. Take their guns away from them and you wouldn't find a real man amongst them.'

She was standing silhouetted before the window again. Neeley was having a tough time concentrating.

'You'd better come on down, Rhea.'

'Oh, very well,' she said petulantly. 'Tell him I'll be there in five minutes . . . possibly naked!'

Neeley vanished with his message. But Rhea was not down in five minutes. The blue didn't suit, so she tried the purple. Too dramatic. She tried another. It finally took her husband's impatient shout from downstairs to draw her from the room.

'What the blazes have you been doing?' Wardlaw shouted from halfway up the winding staircase. 'Didn't Neeley tell you that—'

He broke off as she appeared at the head of the stairs. In a simple pink check dress with a ribbon in her hair, she looked far too beautiful for a man to want to argue with. So Wardlaw stopped scowling and instead extended his hand with a forced smile.

'Come on, I would really like you to meet this fellow, my dear. Quite a surprise, really, even to me.'

Sarcastic responses sprang to her mind but the rich man's wife chose to remain silent as they descended the staircase hand-in-hand, creating a perfect picture of style, grace and self assurance. And of course, wealth. Strikes, fluctuating minerals prices, or rival miners and tycoons notwithstanding, Foley Wardlaw was still very much *numero uno* in this troubled town and he insisted that both he and Mrs

Wardlaw should always look the part.

They entered the room together.

Coe Neeley was seated at Wardlaw's desk while the only other man present stood with his back to the room as he gazed over the rolling lawns and carefully tended gardens beyond.

He was not overly tall but powerfully built for a gunfighter. He turned as the couple entered. Expecting to encounter features twisted by violence and cruelty, Rhea was taken aback to find herself staring at a face of striking handsomeness and no little arrogance as she felt herself weighed, examined and possibly even judged by expressionless dark eyes.

And then her husband was performing the introductions: 'Mr Coder . . . Mrs Wardlaw.'

She nodded distantly. Next moment she was taken aback when the gunfighter stepped forward and took her hand.

'My pleasure, Mrs Wardlaw.'

She was offended; who would not be? She felt he held her hand a moment too long. She wanted to pull away but there seemed almost something hypnotic in his steady look. *Probably some abnormality in vision caused by all the dead people he's seen?* she mused. Then tugged her fingers free and stepped back to claim her husband's arm.

'How do you like our town?' she asked formally, attempting to patronize him with her faked politeness. 'Mr Coder?'

'I haven't made up my mind. I haven't seen that

much of it yet.'

'Did you happen to pass the graveyard on the way in?'

'Now, Rhea!' Wardlaw protested sharply. He smiled at Coder. 'My wife and I have different views on some matters ... peacekeeping and rabble-control for instance. But all that can wait for another time. You must be weary after your long ride, Coder. I've arranged to have you lodged here at the mansion with us, as a large part of your duties will be our protection. Your quarters are in the east wing in the old maids' section. Er, Rhea, would you find Abigail and have Mr Coder shown to his quarters?'

But Rhea Wardlaw would not be dismissed so easily.

'Is it true, as I'm led to understand it, Mr Coder, that you kill people for a living?'

The room went quiet but Coder appeared unfazed as he turned his hat in his hands and met her eyes levelly.

'When I must.'

'And how often might that be?'

'As often as somebody tries to break the law and I can prevent it.'

'Oh, I understand.' Her tone was sarcastic. 'You are not really a killer-for-hire but actually a lawman in disguise?'

Wardlaw scowled darkly. 'Damnit, Rhea, if you can't be civil you might at least not go out of your way to be downright offensive.'

34

'I don't bruise easy, Wardlaw,' Coder said quietly, studying the woman. 'The truth is, Mrs Wardlaw, there are a lot of men like me who do the work of the law even though they might work outside it. There's never enough law to go around in the West, as you likely know. We help fill up some of those gaps.'

'By filling graves, you mean?'

That was enough for Foley Wardlaw. Shedding his charm like a cloak he clapped his hands loudly and a manservant appeared instantly from a corridor.

'George, Mrs Wardlaw is feeling the heat and would like to be shown to her chambers!' He swung back sharply as his wife made to protest, and Coder saw in that moment that Foley Wardlaw was a dangerous man behind his polished looks and style. 'You will permit George to see you to your rooms – madam! I mean now!'

Coder half expected fireworks from the woman. But there were none. Rhea Wardlaw was feisty and outspoken by nature, and her husband at times suspected her of infidelity. But she was not stupid, nor did she underestimate Wardlaw's total ruthlessness when crossed or challenged.

So she coolly draped her stole over one shoulder, gave the gunfighter an aloof nod and followed the servant along the corridor to vanish from sight.

Coder was not taken in by Wardlaw's wide smile as footsteps faded into silence.

'Ahh, the women ... God bless 'em, eh, Mr Coder?' A heavy and surprisingly powerful hand clapped the gunfighter's right shoulder. 'If only domestic problems were the only kind we menfolk must deal with, eh? But unfortunately if a man intends to build big and hold onto it all he must be prepared for the vicissitudes that make our way more difficult than it rightly should be, and simply take steps to deal with them. Are you with me, sir?'

'I guess.' Coder was still trying to get his head around 'vicissitudes'. 'Are you saying—'

'I'm saying that you are hired and I damn well like the cut of your jib, sir,' the other cut him off. 'Neeley, see Mr Coder has all he needs, then make it your business to let the town know how things have changed as of right now. Welcome aboard, Coder.' He nodded curtly then was gone, striding off like a general whose battles were already won.

Ryan Coder had plenty to occupy his thoughts as the servant guided him off to the east wing. There was the tension he'd felt – first upon riding into the town below an hour earlier, then the arrogance and ruthlessness radiated by his new employer, the beauty and aloofness of his employer's wife.

But right now the fast gun from Nogales was most interested in simply seeing his horse properly cared for before heading off to rest up some after the long ride.

From what he'd already seen and sensed here he felt he should keep sharp and ready for anything, working for the Wardlaw dollar. Or maybe that should that be – the Wardlaws? For he already sensed

36

that Rhea Wardlaw, even while playing her role as the dutiful wife, might prove a handful in her own right.

He'd already felt the tension in the strike-bound town on his way through, but planned to go off quietly and unobtrusively, later tonight alone to take a far more comprehensive look at Sedalia and form his own opinions.

But rest came first.

Within minutes of stretching out upon the big comfortable bed with its lingering scent of delicate perfume, the gunfighter from Nogales was sleeping and dreaming of peaceful times, pretty weather and all those gentle things he never seemed to encounter in his real and wakeful life as a man of the gun.

Only in his dreams.

Every Saturday night they rolled up to the old Pontoon Dance Palace on the south edge of town where the river ran slow and clear beneath the pylons.

They arrived walking or horsebacking along the dusty furrowed road that looped past the closed-down mines. They came in gaudy cheap garb, the hardy miners with rough-stubbled brown faces and slicked-down hair, the women and girls sporting gaudy floral dresses worn with sandals and hand-knitted shawls. Uptown was for the high-rollers and those lucky folks still with jobs. But down here it was just someplace where the unlucky and the lost could get together for next to nothing, sink a few cheap shots and dance and sing their troubles away – if just for a few short hours.

Saturday night there was always a band of some kind, some good, some terrible, but after a few stiff ones at the long plank bar and a twirl around the pontoon floor floating on the water it could seem the music was the equal of anything you might hear in the big cities like Dunstan or Moore's Creek.

Owner Tom Prince had opened the place in '73 and it was still going strong that summer when the big strikes had begun. Now poor folks came in even greater numbers once a week just to have a good time and help forget their kids were half-starving, or that it was beginning to look more and more likely the strikers would be forced to give up their protest eventually and return to the mines under the same harsh conditions as before.

But at least on Saturday nights you got to unwind despite a rumor the strikers were planning a protest march on the Wardlaw mansion, or that Wardlaw had boosted his gun strength both to protect himself and help keep the strikers in line.

But most rumors here often proved to be fiction or fantasy while the here-and-now simplicity of the Saturday night open air dance at the pontoon was real – so let's have some fun and give Old Man Worry the elbow at least for tonight!

Tom Prince never closed his doors before daylight Sunday morning and long before then there was always a fight or sometimes several, but at least one virtually guaranteed.

The night's first brawl erupted at around eleven and it was no surprise that Limehouse Jack was involved. He was the six-foot-six bare-knuckle champion from Old England who would beat up on anyone, who ogled other men's women, swore all the time and drank too much and in general tested the patience of everyone from Tom Prince down to the sawdust boy long before the night was through.

Three striking miners went after the roaring giant together out in the open beneath the moon and the resulting ruckus was in full progress when the stranger in town inobtrusively eased his way into the rickety supply-shed-cum-dancehall and was soon to be seen twirling in the shadows with Kitty from the Red Wall Saloon.

For a time the four-piece band sounded no better than average until Tom Prince jumped onto the bandstand and started in conducting long enough to get them fired up again, by which time the brawling outside appeared to have petered out. Eventually, a swaggering Limehouse showed again, boasting of yet another victory to his hangers-on before shoving a girl's partner aside and grabbing her up for the vigorous two-step.

Coder paid the giant no attention and continued to stand quietly in the shadows for the change-your-partners, aware that he was simply quietly enjoying himself for the first time in – he couldn't recall how long.

He'd quit the Wardlaw mansion without informing anyone, intent on getting the feel of his new town right off and in his own way.

He knew there could be some risk in mixing with the very people who were suffering most both from the strike and Wardlaw's uncompromising attitude to their claims. But he wasn't expecting trouble and was having a fine anonymous time, so lingered on, unaware he had attracted unwanted attention from over by the bandstand.

When the dance finished Coder escorted Kitty back to her friends then breasted the bar where Tom Prince served him personally with a shaking hand.

'Er, this on the house, mister,' the man stammered. 'That is if you take it with you and go – nothing personal, mind.'

Coder put a stare on the man. Plainly he was scared. He turned to search for the source and realized the man called Limehouse was standing staring with his bunch a short distance away across the dance floor, glaring at him intently.

Instinct warned he'd stayed on maybe one dance too long.

Coder flipped Prince a coin, tasted his beer then turned and headed for the exit. He was halfway there when the big voice boomed out.

'Just a bleeding minute there, matey!'

He knew it was the giant. He kept on and almost made it to the doors before two bruisers moved to block his path. He halted and turned slowly to see

Limehouse Jack striding towards him, flexing his giant shoulders and radiating hostility.

'Let's be having a look at you, boyo!' the Englishman growled. 'Feller here claims he seen you up on Wardlaw Hill earlier, mixing with the enemy, so he says.'

Limehouse halted before Coder with fists on hips, as big a man as Coder had ever seen.

'By jingo but up close I swear you sure got the look of one of them gutless back-shooters Wardlaw's been trying to sign on recent. You wouldn't by any chance be that butcher from Nogales we been hearin' rumors about lately, would you? What was that name again, boys?'

'Coder,' somebody supplied.

'Coder . . . yeah, that's it!' Limehouse leaned closer to stare into Ryan's face. Then he looked him up and down until his gaze focused on the shell belt and tied-down gun. The man's eyes flared menacingly as he raised a fist the size of a pie melon. 'By the devil himself I can smell the breed – hired butchers all stink the same. But by God and by Judas I'll not be standing by again and watch one more of your dirty kind put honest hard-working men in their graves—'

That was as far as Coder let him go. The situation was already dangerous with hard-faced men closing in on him while dancers and their partners edged away. The music tinkled to a sudden stop.

As he glanced around he sensed rather than saw Limehouse loom closer and cock a huge fist, plainly intending to go for the 'king hit', the coward's blow that came without warning.

He had no intention to brawl for no reason, wouldn't risk injuring the right hand his life so often depended upon.

A gasp went up at the way the Colt .45 appeared in his fist and men were backing away as he took one long stride towards Limehouse – who refused to give ground. Instead the man bellowed and was swinging a huge fist when the butt of Coder's revolver smashed into his forehead with a sound like an axe biting wet wood.

For a moment it seemed that terrible blow would have little effect. With crimson pouring down his features, Limehouse seemed to be reaching for Coder, until he side-stepped. The giant kept lurching blindly straight past him as if he was on tram tracks, unseeing, possibly out to it, yet still tottering forwards.

Coder kicked his huge legs out from under him and he fell like a California redwood with a crash that shook the building. As Coder turned away his pathway to the doors was suddenly wide open with hard men and pretty dancers alike backing up to get the hell out of the way of the stranger with a naked gun in his fist.

Without a glance at the motionless hulk on the boards he backed up to the doors unchallenged behind his .45. Then he was gone.

Revellers claimed later that it was a full minute

before anybody found the nerve to go outside for fear that Wardlaw's new enforcer might still be around.

Only then did someone go looking for Doc Doolin.

Coder rode slowly for the great house on the hill, thinking: maybe he'd won the first round here but likely nothing had really changed.

Tomorrow the mines would still be locked down, hungry strikers would march rowdily down Main toting their tattered banners, likely to clash with Wardlaw's Regulators before the day was out. Battles between half-starved mining men and the owners' enforcers would rock this beleaguered town yet again.

It all seemed inevitable, like death and taxes.

Sooner or later Coder figured he would be called upon to play an active role in the ugly game with outcomes nobody could guess at. But for now he would breathe easy, go hunt himself up a stiff shot at the mansion, then turn in and and reflect upon everything he'd already learned here.

He would study the Wardlaws with their arrogant ways, sort out the good from the bad in the town, then set out to separate the genuine danger men from those boozing braggards you'd strike in any town, who could mostly be relied upon to fold up the moment things grew serious.

He was expert at assessing a town. Any town.

For he had hired his guns in some places where compromise could not be reached and where towns had erupted into total chaos highlighted by sudden death and raging guns. He had stood by too many times watching the hearses rolling by on their way to Boot Hill, and hoped Sedalia might prove to be different.

He stripped his job here down to the simple basics. Protect Wardlaw and help control the striking Cousin Jacks on the streets and eventually get them back down underground working in the shafts where they belonged.

Yet already instinct and experience combined to warn him that hearses might roll here in troubled Sedalia, that graves could fill and women would weep. The one thing he never allowed himself to foresee, as a proud man of the guns, was that one of those one-way journeys up to Boot Hill could ever be his own.

He hoped to quit his lethal trade before it killed him.

CHAPTER 4

TROUBLE TOWN

Next day was thick with dust and heat, the sun already hot by nine.

Ryan Coder sat in the shade of the hotel veranda in a cane-bottomed rocker watching the town in the early morning. There were few people abroad as yet, merely a scatter of early morning women with shopping baskets over their arms, the odd overhung booze-hound waiting for the saloons to open and a pair of out of work clerks from one of the mines drifting past listlessly and flinching nervously when a trio of brute-faced miners tramped by.

The miners sighted him instantly; he was hard to overlook up there on the high porch. They paused to whisper amongst themselves, unshaven and scowling yet at the same time, subdued. Coder traded stare for stare, waiting for understanding to hit home. First came their awareness that he didn't scare, and next the sudden realization of just how dangerous he looked sitting there all alone with only that big six-gun buckled to his thigh for company.

'Smart move, boys!' he called after them when they suddenly hurried on. None responded.

Coder leaned back and smiled. He knew that breed could be cruel and dangerous. You expected that. Yet they posed but a minor threat to a gun pro. It was the other sort you watched for; the cool breed with a tied-down Colt .45 and 'the look.' Sometimes that look could belong to a hulking six-footer who shaped up like a ploughman yet who could clear and draw faster than a jittery lightweight. Then there was the quiet loner who often dressed in black and always positioned himself someplace where his back was covered and he could watch everybody at once in safety. That breed could seem highly strung and over-cautious, yet still prove so blisteringly fast a man could scarce believe it.

There was none of the danger kind to be sighted on the streets of Sedalia this early, nor did he expect there to be. It was his experience that when someone like himself first showed up in a town the profession-als stepped back and took their time assesssing you first, weighing your worth and trying to decide if you would prove to be just another overblown phoney or maybe the real thing.

Those were the ones to watch.

He stretched and flexed powerful arms. The clat-ter of dishes and cutlery from the dining room in back of him reminded him he'd not eaten yet. He rose and moved to the edge of the veranda to stand there for a time, meeting every passer-by with an expressionless eye, playing out his intimidating role as Wardlaw expected him to do.

Likely the word was already out: new gun in town!

The water wagon rumbled along Main with the driver sitting hunched in his seat, his long whip over his shoulder. The tank was rusty, and the dribbles of water leaking out from the holed pipe behind wouldn't lay the dust for more than an hour before it would need damping down again.

As the rig receded he sighted a house servant from the mansion approaching along the walk. She hailed him. Mr Wardlaw wished to see him over breakfast. It was not an invitation but an order and the gunfighter from Nogales knew it.

Over a meal of cold cuts and hot coffee Wardlaw was eager to hear his impressions of the town, what he'd already learned of the ongoing situation and his assessment of it.

'Well, I've picked up some more on the strikers, and your troubles with saloon-keeper Ace Deagan,' he supplied. 'Anybody else I should keep a special lookout for?'

'Maybe one or two,' Wardlaw said, rising to move about, sipping on his joe. 'Glede Skelley – he's the leader of the strikers and has something like eight of their section bosses backing him. Calls himself an idealist, but I don't.'

'Dangerous?'

'Not really. Dangerous would fit his friend, Toby John. He doesn't look much but he's got money and quite a following – and he hates my guts.'

'Anyone else I should know about?'

'Mainly only Deagan, the saloon-keeper. He does-n't have numbers but he certainly possesses money, power and the ambition to go with it, which can be highly dangerous in the hands of that breed.'

'I figure I can understand the miners' angle. If they got rid of you there'd be a power vacuum and likely they could see themselves filling it. But where would this Deagan profit if you were no longer around?'

'Deagan was born dirt poor and came up the hard way. From the jump he's been obsessed with getting his greedy paws on my mines. This strike trouble was made to order for him and I half suspect he might have helped kick it off himself.'

He paused to shrug.

'The way I see it that saloon-keeper is prepared to stand back and stir the pot until it boils over, then take over the mines when I'm either dead or gone.'

'Could he succeed?'

Wardlaw shrugged.

'As you pointed out to my wife, Coder, out here it's the strongest and the fastest. You see, if I was forced out or killed then the Motherlode and the Birdcage Mines would pass on either to my wife or the Company. But neither would be strong enough to hold out against Deagan. But all along I've held my own against him, which is why he now feels he's got to get me out of his way.'

'And this Toby John you mentioned?'

The tycoon grimnaced.

'He's an ornery gold and silver miner who struck it rich in California then settled down here to drink himself to death. He despises the ruling class and is obsessed with bringing me down and seeing his miners take over. Naturally, he's got plenty support and is full of hate, maybe even a little touched in the head. According to Slater he's been agitating the strikers to set fire to my house and hang me on Main.'

'Nobody will get to do that while I'm here.'

Wardlaw smiled and glanced at Coe Neeley. 'I'm certain we have the right man here.'

'Reckon so,' murmured Neeley, sounding anything but enthusiastic.

Wardlaw frowned at the man. 'Anything wrong?'

Neeley glanced obliquely at Coder then shook his head. 'Nothing at all, Mr Wardlaw.'

Wardlaw continued talking but Coder was no longer paying attention. Neeley puzzled him. The two had seemed to hit it off during the long ride from Nogales, yet here the man seemed to have been growing more and more distant, particularly whenever Rhea Wardlaw was about.

Coder came sharply alert when knuckles rapped on the door. A blocky, broken-nosed man with the unmistakable swagger of a gun came in with big spurs jingling.

'Ah, Slater,' said Wardlaw. 'Meet Ryan Coder from Nogales.'

The gunfighters exchanged cool nods, sizing each other up.

'You'll be working together,' Wardlaw explained, 'so I'd like to see you get along – which isn't always the case with you gunmen, so I've observed.'

'Have you explained the new set-up to him?' Coder asked flatly.

'And what set-up might that be?' Wardlaw wanted to know.

'The one that says I'm running things now,' Coder stated, causing Slater to flush and shoot a questioning look across at Wardlaw.

'Well, I haven't informed him in so many words,' Wardlaw replied. 'As a matter of fact I don't recall actually saying you would be in charge, Coder. I pictured you and Slater and my Regulators working together as a team—'

'It sounds to me like he might have other notions, boss,' Slater cut in.

'You're sharper than you look.' Coder's tone was cold. He turned to Wardlaw. 'You hired me to protect you because of my rep. Well, the reason I've survived so long in this game is that I never rely on another man or his judgement. That's how it will be here. I'll give the orders and Slater and the others will do like I say. That way we might all survive. It's not just a good way to operate – it's my only way!'

Silence.

Hard-eyed Slater was plainly taken aback but was momentarily struck dumb. Wardlaw flushed, feeling his authority was being undermined. Yet almost immediately the big man realized he had felt safer and more secure in just the short time the man from Nogales had been here than he'd done in many months.

That was good enough for Foley Wardlaw. He shrugged and immediately informed Slater that Coder was the new boss of the Regulators.

Slater paled, a hard man with a touchy vanity. He moved to square off before Coder with hands thrust behind gun belt, jaw thrusting.

'A big mouth doesn't make a big man in my book, Coder. And I don't take orders from any overblown rep from the boondocks—'

'You either take orders from me or you're through!' Coder chopped him off.

'Now, gentlemen—' Wardlaw began. But Coder was talking and not listening.

'You don't understand, Wardlaw. I'm not suggesting, I'm telling. This second-rater works for me, not with me. Is that clear?'

This was too rich for Slater. Face burning, the gunner grabbed six-shooter handle only to freeze in mid-draw with all color draining from his face. For Coder had already come clear and the muzzle of the .45 in his fist now rammed the gunner's brawny chest.

Instantly Slater backed up and allowed his Peace-maker to slide back into leather. His face was white. For the first time in his life the man had witnessed true gunspeed as opposed to imitations.

'R-reckon you got a point there, Coder—'

'Mr Wardlaw was almost killed recent due to your carelessness,' Ryan stated flatly. 'I'm here to see he stays alive. Every man on his payroll will do as I say from here on in and be ready to give up his life to protect Mr Wardlaw if that's what's called for. Have you got that?'

Nobody expected tough Slater to take that. Yet it was plain he'd already done so before a sharp yell sounded from outside:

'Hey, boss! They're coming up the hill, goddamnit. Two dozen dirty Cousin Jack miners – what game are the mongrels playing now?'

Nobody saw Coder quit the room but already he was striding out onto the great gallery which offered the sobering sight of an untidy swarm of rough-garbed mining men trudging up Wardlaw Hill from the town.

Without hesitation or support he strode out onto the emerald lawns ready to to meet them.

'Judas Priest!' Wardlaw gasped. 'What's he think he's doing? He could get himself killed—'

'You mean – if he doesn't turn to water like the rest of you are doing so shamelessly?' a mocking voice sounded from the stairs.

Wardlaw whirled. His wife had paused halfway

down the spiral stairs. He could tell she'd been drinking but that was often the case these days. Rhea appeared cynically amused by the dangerous situation, and he was about to chide her when a distant shout from the ranks of the miners diverted his attention.

'Damned woman!' he muttered and strode out onto the gallery to realize how much closer the mob was by this. Close and potentially very menacing.

He propped and the others halted behind him. Rhea's mocking laughter sounded.

'Your big moment is at hand, darling! Better not allow your new knight errant grab all the glory! Go forth, my brave husband – seize the moment!'

Wardlaw ignored the taunt. Then he sighted the broad-shouldered figure of Coder standing impassively before the now-slowing threat from below, and taking heart, promptly strode forward.

'Follow me!' he bawled with renewed authority, and the hands with no choice reluctantly trailed him out beneath open skies to fan out on either side of the Nogales gunman, and in a line confronted together one of the ugliest sights on the earth – the face of the mob.

Fierce and crochety little Toby John was panting heavily from the climb as he shot a glance back over his shoulder.

'They never had no real guts and you can see they ain't got it now, Skelley,' he panted, swabbing his overheated face as the pace of the marchers behind slowed even more noticeably now. He squinted back upslope to the carefully tended green lawns and billowing flower gardens of Wardlaw Hill. 'And today's going to prove one of them times or I'm a jackass!'

'What the hell are you griping about now, Toby?' growled Skelley, a serious, middle-aged miner with the history of thirty years underground written clearly in the pallid complexion and permanently bowed back. 'I agreed to bring the boys up here with me to back you up, didn't I? Damnit, what more do you want?'

John, a half-crippled little figure with a gollywog shock of uncontrollable red hair, snorted peevishly.

'You're only planning to do the job by halves, like you always do. You are coming up here to ask Wardlaw to listen to our demands and to protest against this stinking new killer of his. But you should be telling the rich bastard! You can't force any man do nothing unless he respects you. And how is Wardlaw going to respect us when we come up without any guns, like you insisted? Well, his pack of hardcases will be packing iron, make no mistake about that.'

Skelley made no reply, yet knew what John said was likely true.

And in truth Skelley was already regretting his decision to join the protest march. He'd done this at John's insistence after realizing Wardlaw had upped the ante in the ongoing conflict by importing a renowned gunfighter to strengthen his hand against the strikers.

But the higher and more slowly their ragged mob climbed now, the stronger was Skelley's conviction that his ban upon the marchers toting weapons today might prove the smartest thing he'd done all day.

The march was Toby John's idea and Skelley had found himself unable to hold the miners back after the little man had fired them up.

John, the former undergrounder who'd gone West to strike it rich in the silver mines of Gardoka, then returned to Sedalia to support the miners in their struggle for improved conditions, was a hot-head and impulsive by nature. Skelley was often forced to give in to John's demands simply because both he and the strikers were relying upon the man's ongoing financial support and generosity simply to survive these days. By Skelley's estimate John had ploughed thousands of dollars into the strikers' funds just over the past month alone, but was now next door to being broke as a result.

He knew Toby John genuinely supported a fair deal for the workers with improved conditions and all the rest of it. But Skelley realized he was driven more by hatred than any other single factor. Mine bosses had worked him like a dog and almost crippled him for twenty years before he struck it rich, and he hadn't missed one opportunity to square accounts ever since.

'Hey!' somebody in back of Skelley suddenly panted, 'Is that there him?'

The mob immediately straggled to a halt, puffing and blowing. Standing alone a short distance away uphill with one boot raised upon the low brick wall forming the border to the lush lawns and gardens encircling the great house, was a broad-shouldered man in tan shirt and sporting a low-crowned black hat.

Before anybody could speak Glede Skelley knew it must be Coder, for the stranger had that certain look that would throw a chill into any honest man.

But just to be doubly sure, he turned his head and called back, 'That him, Limey?'

The towering figure with sweat streaming down his face and a heavy calico strapping across his forehead, was standing well back with huge fists clenched. He seemed too sullen to reply.

'That's him right enough!' another man panted. 'I seen him at the Pontoon Dance Palace last night. That there is Ryan Coder – the geezer who smashed Limehouse!'

His words carried and an angry muttering rose from the sea of angry faces and hungry faces – faces furrowed with the deep lines of anger, want and despair.

And bitter-faced little Toby John seemed angrier than anybody else.

'See what evil breed the rich tyrant is importing to go against us now? Ain't satisfied with hiring street sweepings and bar-room brawlers to attack us. Wardlaw is so fearful of our strength and so bent on forcing us back down the mines to toil for him like animals – he's gone and upped the ante! You can see now that Slater and them other guntippers are just yap-dogs barking, compared to this mongrel, Coder. But united we're more than a match even for a rich man's hired butcher – so show me just what you think of Mister Killer Coder, boys!'

The responding yell which washed over an impassive Coder was all too plainly half-hearted and seemed to affect him not at all. He waited impassively until the sounds subsided before responding.

'You could have saved yourselves the trouble of marching up here, Cousin Jacks! Mr Wardlaw has nothing to say to any mob now or at any time. If you want to go about this civilized and choose a spokesman then maybe something might be arranged—'

'Who gave you the right to act as spokesman?' an angry voice challenged. 'Git movin' and go tell that rich mongrel to stop hiding behind his wife's skirts and come listen to what we workers got to say. We sure ain't dealing with no dirty Nogales back-shooter!'

A ragged yell of support greeted this. Coder's only response was a slight nod as he lowered his right hand to rest on the handle of the .45 in its cutaway leather holster. This caused an involuntary surge backwards before a hurled rock clattered upon house tiles, causing the chanting to start up again.

'We want Wardlaw! We want Wardlaw!' They roared, and Coder turned to glance up at his employer standing pale upon the front gallery.

Eventually, the big man came down the wide steps to make his unhurried way across the lawn to stand at Coder's side, grim-jawed and defiant. A brawny striker emitted a curse and made to step across the low brick barricade, brandishing a broken bottle.

'Damn you, Wardlaw—' he howled, but got no further. Coder moved in fast to throw a short punch to the jaw that landed with an impact that saw the heavyweight's poor-man hat fly feet into the air.

The man rolled downslope like a log. When Coder straightened, everyone realized the big black Colt had filled his fist as though by sleight-of-hand.

The angry uproar subsided and then died when he thumbed the hammer back onto full cock.

In the deepening quiet his voice carried clearly. 'This caper's over – done and dusted. You will back up, then shut up and listen to what Mr Wardlaw has to say. Either that or take your chances against me.'

He may have been bluffing. Who could tell? Maybe he didn't even know himself. He realized many were afraid. Yet it was plain to his experienced eye that the miners had likely whipped themselves up to a level where they felt they must go on with it, regardless of the risks.

They may have done just that but for the totally unexpected.

It was feisty Toby John who was first to glimpse something unexpected happening beyond Coder and Wardlaw. The runt blinked and elbowed the striker at his side. The man looked and cussed, touching off a rising murmur of voices as every head began to turn.

Coder backed up a step before glancing over his shoulder. He blinked. Rhea Wardlaw was descending the steps from the mansion gallery trailed by several nervously smiling housemaids bearing trolleys and trays of drinks and sweetmeats.

'Foley!' the woman called brightly, as though oblivious to the tension as virtually every eye now focused upon her. 'What on earth is all the fuss about?' Then she stepped lightly past her husband and Coder to reach across the low border and take a dumbfounded Toby John by the hand. 'And where are your manners, darling?' she went on in the same light tone. 'All these good working-men appear quite cross, and I can't say I blame them. Such a long walk in the heat and not a sign of refreshment for anybody – and you and Mr Coder acting so inhospitably. Really! But luckily I just happened to have something prepared – just in case it might be needed today. Come on, girls, don't be shy. Please attend Mr John and Mr Skelley first, they look exhausted.'

Coder still had a hand on gun handle, watching Toby John's hot red face. The man's temper was notorious. But when the little runt stared up into the woman's face and actually half-smiled, he realized it was over. He didn't understand why as yet, but was quick to step back to make way for the housegirls to approach the low barricade and proffer their glasses of wine and cut sandwiches.

Within moments the entire atmosphere had changed dramatically and a small cheer actually went up when a relieved Glede Skelley jumped nimbly up onto the brick wall and held a drink in one hand and a buttered bun in another over his head, then executed a little tap dance, whether in triumph or relief nobody could tell – but it brought a cheer anyway.

For Skelley was no fighting man, while the pick-up bunch which he'd bullied into taking part in the demonstration by Toby John were simple under-grounders who'd marched reluctantly upon Wardlaw Hill acutely aware they were running the risk of getting hurt or even killed.

There was plainly no chance of this happening now as they watched Rhea actually squeeze little Toby John's hand and turn the full candlepower of her smile upon the hunch-shouldered little runt, who seemed too dazzled even to cuss.

Then, 'Your glass, Mr John. I'll share it with you and perhaps we can all sit down comfortably like sensible people and discuss what it is you men really want – and what we might do to help. Then you can tell me how your sciatica is these days.'

This was the first hint anybody had that John and Wardlaw's wife were on familiar terms. But many

sensed it when the crazy little miners' advocate actually managed a smile and accepted the proffered
glass.

'Miz Warlaw,' he toasted, 'I always claimed you
might be on our side, and by glory I declare you've
proved that today. Join me?'

Coder shook his head as he saw the woman slip
one arm through the miner's and they chinked
glasses. Back up on the gallery, flanked by armed
security, a scowling Wardlaw finally dragged his hand
off gunbutt and shook his head, at once relieved yet
somehow also offended by what he was witnessing.
But mostly he was relieved, as was his new bodyguard.

Standing apart from the others Coder continued
to gauge the true temper of the mob until the
muttering and cussing of a mere handful was finally
swallowed up by a pervading air of goodwill, the last
of the tension vaporizing like woodsmoke.

'Why, thank you kindly, ma'am,' a hugely relieved
Glede Skelley yelled loudly. 'From all of us!' That
drew a ragged cheer and he slugged down his
whiskey then swung to face the mansion with empty
glass held high. 'See, Wardlaw, we can be just as civilized as you – but we ain't leaving unless you agree to
talk later, by God!'

'He agrees!'

Everyone stared at Coder, who'd responded.
'That's right!' He ignored the reaction from Wardlaw
as he swung back to face Skelley and Toby John. He
spread now empty hands wide. 'Everybody have a

drink and then Skelley and John will join Mr Wardlaw inside to discuss their problems like sensible folks should.'

He sounded confident but wasn't. This didn't come until Glede Skelley suddenly grinned, strode across to him and extended his hand. The gunfighter and the miners' leader shook, and it was over.

For now.

CHAPTER 5

THE CHALLENGE

Holly squinted upwards then cursed on realizing just how low the sun had fallen. He must have slept two hours! Yet he'd not meant even to doze off, just rest up some until the heat went out of the day and his pards had returned.

The gunslinger sat up sharply and sleeved his mouth. There was no sight of his two pards from Nogales anyplace upon this windy hillside. Nothing to be seen but mesquite, those gaunt and stunted buttes, and— Wait! Wasn't that a cloud of hoof-lifted dust rising above the arroyo a mile higher up?

Fully alert now, the gunslinger grabbed up his field glasses which instantly brought the arroyo jumping into clear vision. He muttered impatiently waiting for the dust to clear then made an adjustment to the screws and refocused. He saw nothing as he played the lenses up and down the twisted scar of the arroyo line before catching a momentary blurred glimpse of moving figures some two miles higher up, heading back downwards.

It could only be Chainer and Spice returning from the Old Dorio site. The diggings were believed to be all mined out and had lain idle for years until three cash-strapped young guns from Nogales had decided to give the worked-out shafts just one last try.

With characteristic high energy, Holly had kicked on well ahead of his henchmen the previous day to explore the region alone. A two-mile climb quickly discouraged him and he was well on his way back before his partners caught up.

Chainer and Spice were still enthusiastic yet were hardly surprised to find Holly had lost interest as he tended to do with just about everything unless it was connected with guns.

The pair had rated Holly as Nogales's *numero uno* with the Colts ever since Coder's quitting to take up that high-paying gun job up in the mining country.

Unlike Holly, Chainer and Spice weren't afraid of getting sensitive gun hands all callused up by hard labor, and were still eager enough to go off together and check out the old mines. They would rejoin him back at the mouth of the arroyo later that night to report on whether they figured the old site worth the effort, or not.

They were like a pair of kids, Holly mused cynically and sneered at their youthful hopping about and acting all excited before vanishing into the jaws of the arroyo. He sneered. They were going to make a big strike. Like hell!

He returned to his camp up on the hillside and played his glasses up and down the arroyo trace for what seemed too long without sighting anything of interest. Might as well get across there and wait for them to emerge, he decided.

A short time later saw him pushing his horse downslope at a walk-trot while checking out his .45.

Holly sighed and scowled.

It was a long time since the youthful gun ace from Nogales had felt really good. Six months earlier he'd been the rising star in the desert hell-hole but since then life had felt like downhill all the way, which he attributed to bad luck, lost chances and his failure to stake his claim as Nogales's number one.

He passionately believed himself to be the fastest of the fast with a list of kills to back that claim. But in his climb for the top he'd kept coming up against Ryan Coder, who seemed destined to continue to rate as *numero uno* until he either died of old age or somebody blew him out of his boots.

Things had been deathly dull in Nogales since Coder had quit it on that big gun job, which was the reason Holly had joined Chainer and Spice when they made the impulsive decision to go gold-hunting instead of hunting men – even if that was the skill at which all three truly excelled.

He stared bleakly at an empty sky and pictured Coder up there amongst those rioting miners, scaring the hell out of everybody and acting out his role as king of the gunfighters while Holly seemed destined to be forever the contender. The kid. . . .

It was almost dark when he reached the arroyo mouth. By the time he'd scouted around and fed both his mount and himself it was pitch black yet with the promise of a moon later on.

Sitting on a blanket smoking one bitter cigarette after another in total darkness in hostile country was a bitch. But at least it kept a man sharp, and he was every bit as alert in that final quarter-hour before moonrise as he'd been an hour earlier – when he heard it.

Up canyon somewhere, not too far distant, a hoof clicked a pebble and then all was death-watch still again.

By that time Holly was invisible in a shallow draw with his .45 in his fist listening to the sounds draw closer.

He told himself it could only be his pards – but a man didn't survive long in this trade by taking chances. His eyes had grown accustomed to the darkness by this and he retained just enough vision to make out the dim shapes of two men emerging from the canyon mouth leading their mounts.

He was about to reveal himself when something caused him to hesitate. It seemed one figure appeared taller than either Chainer or Spice, while the other was plainly bow-legged and thickset and walked like a goddamned Indian!

Still as death he watched and waited while the dim figures put a fire together. As the first flames leapt he realized the squat runt was in truth some kind of breed – who was wearing Spice's gaudy plaid shirt! His companion was a deadly looking gunpacker Holly had never sighted in his life.

Squatting on either side of the fire, relaxed and unawares, the two talked and joked as they rummaged in their knapsacks to produce a collection of boots, guns and hats which the silent watcher identified as belonging to his partners.

He felt a chill on realizing just how close he'd come to revealing himself minutes earlier and likely getting shot to doll rags!

Then cold rage saw him rise and stalk forward until firelight illuminated his lithe figure. The bigger of the two men jerked his head up, choked out a curse and clawed for the pistol in his belt.

Four bullets exploded in his skull before his hand even closed over Colt butt.

The survivor proved lithe as a whippet and was up on two legs with gun in hand before a two-ounce chunk of lead drilled his heart and hurled his body across the fire, setting flames crackling hungrily.

By the time he'd gone through their gear and come up with more of Chainer and Spice's pathetic possessions, Holly was cool again, almost indifferent to what had taken place.

And yet the bloody incident had its powerful effect insofar as, regardless of anything else, it had rammed home the reality of just how vastly the young gun's skills had improved over recent months.

For a long time now he had privately ranked himself as Nogales's *numero uno* with the Colts, the uncrowned fast gun king and *pistolero* without peer – but surely this was the proof!

He was like a man reborn as he stood tall and stared wonderingly up at that gibbous moon rising – and calculated it was just three days' ride to Sedalia.

And knew no contender could claim the kingship until the old king was dead.

Coder fashioned a neat cigarette and lit up as the marching miners appeared from the side street and swung along Main.

The ragged Cousin Jacks might have started out in ranks, and there was still a suggestion of the martial about their denim garb with those tattered red sashes slung across their chests. But there was little else that was in any way impressive or intimidating as they revealed how they had primed themselves for the parade at the saloon when they suddenly erupted into song:

We can be strong together if we stick,
Yes we can, yes we can!
We can out-wait Wardlaw
Or send the bastard broke.
Yes we can – oh, yes we can!

The singing broke off into drunken yelling and there was laughter from onlookers when a red-faced marcher lost his footing and crashed sideways into a waste bin, scaring a horse tethered to the Red Wall's hitchrail, and causing it to rear wildly.

Somebody cheered them from a high window and someone else laughed derisively as they continued on down Main. A marcher in the second rank picked up a rock and hurled it at the courthouse where it disappeared with a tinkle of shattering glass.

'You gonna let 'em get away with that, gunfighter?' a voice demanded at Coder's elbow.

Coder didn't take his eyes from the receding strikers. 'I'm not the law.'

'No? Well from where I stand you gotta be about the closest thing we got to it. Our sheriff ain't got the grit even to talk back to his wife, and them others at the jailhouse ain't even as brave as he is. Don't your boss want 'em to stop this sort of thing?'

He made no response. The marchers weren't his concern any more than was the strike, the hungry kids or the violence that continually erupted between those who still had money here and those who didn't.

All that signified for the gunfighter from Nogales was that Wardlaw was safe and secure in the conference room of the Provincial Bank across the street, and that he was getting hungry.

Yet the mob continued to study him warily as he stood there, for bitter experience had taught them that any strikers' parade could very easily turn into a strikers' drunken riot where bystanders could easily get hurt or maybe even killed. That's how bad things were in strike-ridden Sedalia and could become worse, depending upon the outcome of the meeting taking place across the street right now.

But if the gunfighter from Nogales was aware of the onlookers or their concerns, he gave no sign. He had a job to do and as always would see it done.

The bank's side door finally swung open and some half-dozen figures in miners' rig emerged and started off for the central block, muttering and cussing.

If Coder were a betting man he would wager Skelley and his people weren't heading off to cele-berate any kind of victory over Wardlaw at that meet-ing.

This was confirmed when Wardlaw emerged flanked by Slater and Hunter. As Coder waited for the trio to cross the street to join him, a familiar runty figure emerged from the bank and trudged east along the plankwalk at an uneven shuffling gait.

It was the strikers' spokesman Toby John who turned momentarily to glare across at the gunman, wild-eyed and accusing, so it seemed – or maybe even just a little loco – before the gloom swallowed him.

'How'd it go?' Coder asked Wardlaw as he fell in alongside.

'How do you think it went? I promised everything

and gave them nothing. Like taking candy from a kid.'

Two drunks came weaving towards them. The pair attempted to maintain their place on the plankwalk until Slater and Hunter moved ahead and shouldered them off into the street. The boozehounds cursed and shook their fists after them but the party from the mansion paid no heed as the lights of Main beckoned.

'Toby John looked sore, coming out,' Coder remarked casually.

'So?'

Foley Wardlaw was feeling full of himself tonight. And why not? In just one twenty-four-hour day he'd drawn the teeth of a miners' mob and then tonight had left their leaders with more empty promises and not one single concession.

'Seems I scent trouble,' Coder stated.

'What can they do? Their brats are growing hungrier by the day and within the week the whole pack of them will be begging me to let them back into the mines to work for whatever I want to pay them. That doesn't shape up like trouble to me.'

'Are conditions underground getting worse as they claim?'

'Who cares?'

'Could prove risky – pushing men over the edge. . . .'

Wardlaw propped and stared at him under a Main Street lamp.

71

'Something on your mind, gunfighter?'

Coder gestured. 'I saw men like this in Utah once. Timberjacks. They weren't on strike but they had a grudge against a railroad that had stopped sending in trains for their timber. They were starving too. They ended up burning down the rail depot and tearing up twenty miles of track before the Army got them quietened. They looked a lot like these diggers do tonight.'

Wardlaw laughed and started off again.

'Forget it, Coder. Sheep are sheep and can't—' He broke off. 'Hey, there's Rhea waiting for us. Hey, honey, where are we dining?'

Coder dropped back a pace as Wardlaw strode on ahead to where his wife waited in the brightly-lit lobby of the hotel. By the time they reached the couple Wardlaw had designated an eatery and both insisted Coder join them.

He agreed even though not hungry. His 'victory' over the strikers on Wardlaw Hill seemed to weigh heavy for some reason. Then he mused: *Maybe I really am hungry if I start fretting about the losers in this game. . . .* And decided then and there that the rare steak and speckled gravy Rhea was suggesting to him sounded just fine.

It was as the party headed east along Main that trouble appeared up ahead. A bunch of miners were strung along the gallery of the Feed and Grain Barn as though expecting them to happen by.

Immediately Coder picked up his stride, reaching

72

the building well ahead of the others. He stopped and let his eyes play over the sullen group. He was not surprised to sight Toby John standing on the steps with his ginger thatch catching the street-lamp light. The runty leader glared fiercely at the gun-fighter then turned his head and spat.

'Is this how it is now?' he asked sourly. 'The big man not even game to walk abroad in his own town unless he's got his hog butcher with him?'

'What do you want, John?'

'What do I want? I want what every honest mining man in this town wants, Coder. Simple industrial justice and—'

'Shut your stupid mouth!' Wardlaw was at Coder's side now, suddenly angry. 'Goddamnit, it's bad enough to have you scum trespassing on my private property, now you're harassing me on the public streets.'

'I just want to talk, Wardlaw—'

'We've talked, damn and blast you!' Wardlaw over-rode him. Then, 'Clear them out of my way!' He was speaking to Coder.

Coder shrugged and approached Toby John, who avoided his grasp and started in cursing. A baldy-headed miner with a bristling black beard started down the steps only to run into a sweeping backhan-der from Coder that felled him as if he'd walked into a wall. In the same motion the gunfighter grabbed John by his shoulder and heaved him off the steps to stumble awkwardly and go down.

Still without a word Coder beckoned the party to move on ahead, which they did. He turned back to bark a warning word at Glede Skelley before seizing a dazed Toby John by the collar and hauling him to his feet. The man was shaken yet still able to cuss, but the gunfighter spoke over him.

'Are you crazy, man? You forced this strike, you're all suffering on account of it, and now you've plainly still got the fool notion that hell-raising and rough-housing might fix it. Why do you think Wardlaw hired me? To protect him, you fool, and that's what I will do.'

He shoved the man back against the wall. His next words were for the gaping onlookers.

'I've got one word of advice for you people. Negotiation. That's the single chance you've got to come out of this mess with anything. But keep up this rough stuff and you could force me to quit talking and start in shooting – can't you see that? If that happens you'll have nobody to blame but yourselves and this crazy little bastard you seem to look up to. So, be warned!'

It was a long speech for him but sounded as if he meant every word. Yet by the time he caught up with the others waiting for him a short distance ahead he appeared relaxed.

He glanced back; the miners were staring after him in silence. 'I doubt they'll give us any more trouble tonight. . . .' He looked at the Wardlaws, absently noting what a striking couple they made, sleek,

74

poised and dressed like royalty in such violent contrast with the men he'd just dealt with. 'Did you say the Red Wall?'

Foley Wardlaw nodded. Soon they were seated at the town's top saloon and diner where they settled down to a tolerably pleasant meal with a good wine – without incident or interruption.

Coder ate well but didn't drink. He rarely did when working. After escorting the party back to the mansion on the hill he returned to the central block which he set out to pace slowly to and fro for more than an hour until the lights began to dim and one by one the night-owls, high-rollers and three-time losers drifted off into the night.

At last he stood alone before the abandoned sheriff's office, hands on hips, absorbing the silence. Sedalia was sleeping and yet he was aware of hidden eyes, watching. The town had quietened down for tonight yet a gunfighter's every instinct warned it was still far from peaceful.

CHAPTER 6

CODER'S WAY

'Name your poison, mister.'

'Tequila.'

'Tequila? Say, we don't get much call for that in this man's town. Let me see now – oh, yeah, got me one bottle here. Lemon and salt with it, stranger?'

Coder almost smiled. This gloomy little dive might well be on the outer fringe of town but he didn't believe the bartender wouldn't know who he was. Maybe the man simply wanted to appear neutral and uninvolved. It seemed everybody in Sedalia was taking sides in the conflict these days but plainly there were some, like the barkeep, who were weary of the ongoing violence and tension and simply wanted to keep out of it – if that was possible.

'Lemon and salt,' he affirmed and turned to survey the room. Two ranch hands, a bum or two counting their coins in the hope they'd tally up to the price of a shot, a hostler with a rope over one shoulder and two Regulators from the Motherlode smoking thin cigars over by the west window.

He would like to think this might be a single outpost of calm and common sense in a troubled town, but doubted that was the case. As he sampled his tequila, he could see the barkeep's curiosity over-riding his caution now. The man suddenly snapped his fingers.

'Say, I bet you're that feller they're all talking about—' he began, but Coder was already toting his drink across the room.

The Regulators fell silent and stared up when he stopped at their table. They looked tough and had to be. Their job these days was to keep the mines secure and prevent break-in attempts at vandalism from the locked-out strikers.

Unlike the barkeep, the two didn't pretend not to know who he was. 'Help you?' asked Tolan.

He introduced himself and they responded. Then he said, 'How are the shafts holding up? I hear they've been deteriorating fast during the shut-down?'

'That's so,' said Briggs. 'No maintenance. Mr Wardlaw can't afford to keep repair staff on when no copper's being mined and no revenue coming in.' He paused and puckered his brow. 'Say, you get to see the big man every day, Mr Coder. You reckon he's got any intention of doing a deal with the Cousin Jacks or maybe he just means to bring them to their knees so they end up with no choice but to go back underground on his terms?'

'Hard to say. He doesn't confide in me on matters like that.'

'Hard man that – Mr Wardlaw. . . .'

They were waiting for him to comment, he could tell. That wasn't his style. Wardlaw paid his wages and so warranted his loyalty. But loyalty to the man who paid you was not the same thing as liking or even respect.

'You going back to the Motherlode?' he enquired. They nodded and he went on, 'You want to show me around some? I hear the miners first went on strike on account the maintenance was so bad that men kept getting hurt by tunnel fall-ins and suchlike?'

'Would that make any difference to you if you found it was so?' Tolan asked curiously.

Coder shrugged.

'Likely not,' he conceded. 'But when I deal into a poker game I like to try and get a feel for the cards – all the cards. . . .'

A short time later found him prowling the poorly-lit main shaft of the Motherlode copper mine. He didn't need to be an expert to see that whoever declared the mine dangerous knew his business. Signs of neglect were to be seen on every side; caved-in walls that hadn't been repaired, constant water seepage from the roof, pouring down in some cases. Foul air, bad lighting and a general impression of disrepair all combined to create a deeply depressing picture of neglect and probably danger.

He couldn't help comparing this grim nether-world with all those vast rooms with their twenty-feet ceilings and crystal chandeliers up on Wardlaw Hill.

He was always uncomfortable in enclosed spaces, and breathed easier when back in the daylight on Main Street a short time later. He'd left Tolan and Briggs back at the mine. Their main job these days was to ensure no starving strikers got the chance to vent their spleen upon Wardlaw property.

He was making his way past the City Bank when he realized a rig of some kind was keeping pace with him on the street. He paused, and saw a double-rigged gig from the mansion drawn by a familiar flashy pony, with Rhea Wardlaw plying the reins.

He nodded and the woman reined in and patted the seat beside her. He hesitated a moment before crossing to the vehicle and climbing up.

'Anything wrong?' was his first query.

'Nothing – or everything. Depends on your point of view.' She slapped the lines. 'I've been shopping and my husband is in a meeting, as you know. Are you supposed to be guarding him, or is—?'

'No, he's got Ryan and Walker with him today. Claims they're all he needs by daylight most days when in town. I guess he's right.'

The woman brushed at her hair. She wore it in a different style today, almost covering one half of her face.

'Can I drop you somewhere?'

'Well, I'll ride up to the house with you if that suits. I need to talk with Slater and maybe Neeley if they're about.'

Rhea slapped the lines and the spirited horse broke into a trot. He saw how expertly she steered her way through the light traffic. He'd noted she seemed to do most things well, such as quelling that potentially dangerous situation when John and Skelley led that mob up the hill, looking for trouble or justice – he still wasn't sure which.

And reminded himself he didn't really need to know this either. *You are not paid to think, Coder. Your job is to protect Wardlaw and stay alive yourself. Simple.*

They passed the shabby Miners' Rest building on the way out. Haggard and unshaven men sat listlessly upon the porch, scowling and gesticulating when they realized who it was going past. As they wheeled by he glanced back to see little Toby John rush out into the street after them, eyes blazing and shouting something unintelligible.

Some up at the mansion claimed John was going a little crazy in his conflict with Wardlaw. Maybe they were right.

At last he relaxed. He studied the woman's profile for some reaction to what they'd just seen but there was none. He glanced back over his shoulder to see John still shaking his fist and coughing on their dust.

'I just looked around at the Motherlode,' he stated.

'So?'

He almost smiled. She was plainly in a mood today.

'Total luxury,' he remarked drily.

She glanced at him sharply. 'If that is irony then you're directing it at the wrong person. I have nothing to do with the mines, Foley won't even allow me to go there—' She broke off with a shrug. 'Which I suppose suits me.'

'You suppose, Rhea? Does that mean you'd like to—?'

'Change the subject? Yes, I would. Tell me, how long do you expect to be here?'

They were climbing the hill now.

'No telling.'

'I expect you'll be kept on for some considerable time.' She half-smiled. 'If there's one thing my husband is not short of here it's people with grudges against him who would do him serious harm, if they could. You've probably noticed?'

Coder glanced down at the tiny beads of perspiration glistening in the cleavage between deep breasts. His face remained expressionless when he met her gaze.

'Big men make enemies, little men just sit back and hate everybody, I guess.'

'Do you regard yourself as big or little?'

'Maybe neither. Mostly I just see myself as necessary in places like this.'

'Necessary – and brave. I saw how amazingly calm you were when that mob came up the hill.'

He shrugged.

'I'm paid to be brave.'

'Nobody can be paid to be brave. A person either has courage or doesn't. You have it. I believe my husband was very lucky to secure your services.'

'Glad you feel that way,' he replied, thinking how stiff and formal he sounded. Then they were rolling to a halt before the front gallery where two house servants hurried down the steps to hand their mistress down.

It was at that moment when Rhea Wardlaw's silky tresses that had covered half her face fell back and he glimpsed the dark bruising to the cheekbone. Unaware of his attention Rhea fingered her hair back into place and made her way toward the marble steps.

His frown cut deep. If he were a betting man he would wager the woman had been struck by some-body.

Coder jumped down and glanced back at the sprawling town before heading inside. Preoccupied with his thoughts he didn't see the deep backward glance Rhea Wardlaw directed his way from the veranda before vanishing inside.

But somebody else saw it.

Coe Neeley stood concealed behind the drawing room drapes smoking a cigarette. Wardlaw's mines manager and right-hand man had been impressed by the way the gunfighter had handled the situation the day the miners marched on the mansion. Yet for personal reasons Neeley still reckoned hiring the gunfighter had been a mistake. How come? Simple. The man felt the boss man's wife appeared far too interested in the gunslinger from Nogales.

That suspicion had struck home mere moments before when he'd glimpsed the way Rhea had glanced back at Coder as he was alighting from the buggy. For before Coder had come to Wardlaw Hill, that was just the way she had once looked at him.

That night Ryan Coder didn't quit the mansion until he'd first escorted Foley Wardlaw home along with several big business associates that he had in tow. The rowdy group quickly took over the front ground-floor rooms where the regular headquarters body-guards on duty took over responsibility for the big man's safety.

That left him free for what was left of the night.

A half-hour later saw him shoulder his way through the batwings of the Red Wall Saloon, whose propri-etor was Ace Deagan, reputedly one of Sedalia's most powerful citizens, a business rival and no friend of Foley Wardlaw's.

From what Ryan observed Deagan and Wardlaw were too much alike to be anything but enemies. Both were ruthless go-getters with fat bankrolls and quiet consciences who clashed with one another and shared little in common, other than the hatred and bitterness each had attracted in his climb toward the top of the heap in the two-fisted frontier town.

'First, know thine enemy.'

That was always Coder's precept when taking on any gun job. But thus far he'd not had reason to focus upon Deagan any more than one of any other half-dozen high-rollers in the town. So he was feeling pretty much at ease as he sampled his tequila and set out to absorb the mood, get the feel of things here at the bright and gaudy Red Wall.

And Honeychile seemed exactly the right place to start.

She was petite and blonde and seemed too young to have yet acquired that brittle hardness which so often went with the trade of drinks hustler and good-time girl. She posed prettily for him beneath a huge pink nude oil painting hanging above the dimly lighted Lucky Cuss Bar.

'There's real gals here if you'd prefer them, hand-some,' she smiled when he paused to gaze up the glowing portrait. 'I'm Honeychile, and I guess everyone knows you are that famous gunfighter feller – right?'

A small smile creased Coder's mouth as he leaned an elbow on the bartop.

'Tennessee?' he guessed.

'Close. Georgia.'

'Ryan.'

'You gonna buy Honeychile a shot, Ryan?'

'I'd like to,' he said, glancing around the lushly appointed room. 'But maybe your boss mightn't like you getting friendly with me?'

'Why not, honey?'

'Well, mainly on account of who I work for. And don't say you don't know I'm on Wardlaw's payroll?'

'Sure, everybody and his brother knows that by now.

But you don't have to worry none about Mr Deagan. He'll do business with anybody who's got the price of a shot on him – even including big, bad gunslingers.'

He decided he liked her. Most here either avoided him or treated him very warily.

'In that case, what are you drinking?' he smiled.

'Why, whatever you are, handsome.'

'Maybe not? I drink tequila.'

She snapped her fingers at the bartender. 'Two tequilas, Barney. Now tell me honest, Mr Coder, did you come here to shoot my boss or not?'

Coder laughed, something he rarely did. But the girl was fresh and cheeky. And when she winked at him as he tasted his tequila, he said, 'I'm not here to blast anyone, girl. But on account your boss and my boss don't hit it off I need to size him up some so's I'll know if he's dangerous or not should big trouble break, is all.'

'Well, here comes your big chance,' she replied, and indicated the inner door which swung open to reveal three men who stared directly across at them. She sighed as if anticipating the trouble he'd hinted at now.

'That's Ace in the Prince Albert. Good-looking cuss, ain't he?'

'I guess so,' Coder agreed, assessing the tall dark man with the pencil-line mustache. 'Who are the others?'

'The next one coming out is Spade Hood, and the giant is—'

'Don't tell me, I already know,' Coder said as the third man moved into the light – six and a half feet tall and built like a Mississippi ferryboat. The bandaging still wrapped around his head contrasted starkly with the angry flush on the giant's face.

Limehouse Jack didn't appear any friendlier here than at the Pontoon Dance Palace.

'S'pose most everyone knows Limehouse,' the girl said innocently. 'He's a famous bare-knuckle fighter Ace imported from Kansas City, and he figures to make a fortune out of managing him. You be especial careful of that one, Ryan Coder honey.'

He nodded and with a, 'Good luck, pretty girl,' motioned her away then straightened from the bar as the trio approached.

He ignored Limehouse and met the saloon-keeper's stare levelly. Up close, Ace Deagan appeared both handsome and hard.

'You won't need your hired help, Deagan,' Coder assured. 'I'm here to talk, not raise the dust.'

'I'll more than raise dust—' Limehouse threatened, but the saloon-keeper silenced him with a gesture. Deagan frowned as he studied Coder at close range.

At length he shrugged and leaned an elbow on the bar top. 'I heard what happened at the Pontoon the other night.' Then he shrugged. 'That's nothing to me, so I guess you'd better take a walk, Limey. We've got things to discuss – me and this bad gunfighter.'

The giant glowered at Coder and tapped his head

bandaging significantly with a forefinger before turning and moving off, growling like a big dog.

The saloon had fallen silent. Deagan jerked his head at the second man who also moved off to leave the two men alone.

'All right, Coder, what brings you here to my place? I know it ain't any social visit. I mean, how could it be with you hiring your shooter to Wardlaw?'

'Well, seeing as you brought it up, let's say I stopped by to warn you personal to keep well clear of Wardlaw. Simple enough?'

Deagan studied him intently then turned his head and spat. 'Maybe we'd better continue this in private? My office?'

'The boardwalk.'

'All right, damnit, the boardwalk,' the man snapped and led the way out through the swinging doors.

The moment they were outside they faced off, Deagan suspicious and angry, Coder virtually expressionless.

'So, what's this jaw about Foley Wardlaw, Coder? I never trouble him nohow.'

'Maybe you don't, maybe you do. But somebody's been looking to harm him recent, and I was hired to see they don't succeed. I'm handing out fair warnings to anybody who might try anything that I won't let it happen.'

'Ahh – so you're not a cheap killer for hire after all? Just a simple honest bodyguard?'

Coder remained unruffled. 'That's right. But somehow you sound like you don't believe that?'

The saloon-keeper's face turned harder. 'That's on account I know Wardlaw. He's the most ruthless bastard in Chad Valley, while I'm a business rival who packs plenty weight. We've been enemies right from the jump and now he's decided he wants me out of the way. So, I got a big hunch he might've hired you to take care of that job. But if that's so, you'd better know it won't be easy.'

Coder nodded. This man was plainly ambitious and dangerous. You could always tell. This didn't faze him.

'You're wrong, Deagan,' he replied quietly. 'But maybe there's no point in trying to convince you of that. So I'll keep it simple. Hands off Wardlaw – or it could cost you your life.'

'You through?'

'All through.'

'OK, now I'll give you a word of advice. Get the hell out of Sedalia while you still can. There's scores of men in this town with one reason or another for wanting Wardlaw dead. Did you know that as soon as the miners called their strike he locked down the shafts and is now trying to starve them into coming crawling back to work for the same old lousy money. In other words, he's a total bastard, and sooner or later somebody will catch up with him whether you're around or not. He's got enemies coming out of his ears and not even a hotshot guntipper can watch everybody all of the time.'

'That's some speech,' Coder replied, turning to go. 'But it doesn't change a thing. Should anything happen Wardlaw, just pray you've got a watertight alibi.'

He turned and headed away.

Halting half a block farther along the plankwalk he glanced back to see Deagan out front and staring after him. The saloon-keeper was flanked on either side by Limehouse Jack and Spade Hood.

He massaged his jaw thoughtfully as he moved on. There could be no doubting Wardlaw was hated in Sedalia, any more than you could deny Ace Deagan was a dangerous man, plainly with plenty backing. When you linked Deagan up with all those Wardlaw-hating miners it added up to a sobering picture of what could prove one of his toughest assignments.

His jaw set and he resolved from here on in he would sleep with one eye open in this troubled town named Sedalia.

Federal Street was in sharp contrast to the color and bustle of Shotgun, which Coder had just put behind him.

Abruptly, there were clusters of miners' shacks and hovels all jammed on top of one another on either side of what was more a twisted and muddy track than a made-up street. Here it was hessian at the windows, slush puddles in the streets and patches in the pants. The smell that hung over Federal was the stink of poverty while the eyes that stared out dully at his passing figure held only resentment and hatred. Not because of who he was maybe but more likely because he simply had a full belly while they were growling hungry.

A skinny urchin directed him to Glede Skelley's house. Well before he got there the whisper had gone up that 'Wardlaw's killer' was in the quarter. He passed by unhurriedly through piles of rubble and around trash heaps, matching stare with stare, his obvious lack of fear likely his best protection.

He found Skelley hunched on a bench on his back porch, wrangling with Toby John. The miners' spokesman was distant and suspicious at first but relaxed some when he learned about Wardlaw's invitation to parley with him next day.

'You hear that, Toby?' Skelley grinned, shaking John by a scrawny shoulder. 'This is the ray of sunshine I told you would shine through sooner or later.'

Toby John shook the hand away, appearing more than ever like a gollywog with his tangle of odd-colored hair and that unnerving, black-eyed stare.

'You were always too easily led, Skelley,' the man said bitterly. 'Can't you see this here butcher-boy and Wardlaw have been cooking up some fresh treachery between them aimed at destroying us all! It's a dirty trick and stinks to high heaven.'

'It's no trick, Skelley,' Coder insisted. 'We can't promise anything will come of the meeting but it's got to be a step in the right direction.'

'I reckon maybe you're right about that. Surely you can agree, Toby?'

'I can't do nothing of the sort,' retorted ever-angry John. 'I know Wardlaw's breed. All they're interested in is working an honest man to death then flinging him into the trashbin when he can't work good any more. They're all the same and any man who reckons different is a goddamned fool. There's only one way with this breed – bring them to their knees any which way you can, then make them give you your rights!'

Coder studied the man thoughtfully as he continued to rant. He was aware that the outburst was carrying over the rooftops and soon attracted a crowd of strikers who drew warily closer to lean upon Skelley's rickety back fence.

Maybe Coder could understand John's bitterness and frustration. Yet, as before, he also sensed the man's borderline craziness. This brought to mind Wardlaw's provision regarding Toby John.

'You've got a right to your own ideas, mister,' he stated flatly. 'But they're not ideas that are likely to help bust this strike and get the mines working again.' He turned back to Skelley. 'That's why Wardlaw told me to tell you John's banned from this meeting. Do you agree to that condition?'

Toby John leapt up with a spray of curses. It took a time for Skelley to quieten him down before he eventually turned and nodded to Coder. He was in agreement.

Ignoring John's flamboyant temper tantrum, Coder gravely shook hands on the deal with Skelley, touched hatbrim and headed for the gate.

A sullen avenue opened for him through the miners' ranks.

Amongst the sea of bitter faces he glimpsed a husky youth he'd sent home earlier. Now the young man grinned uncertainly. Coder nodded gravely and continued on. Yet he was encouraged, and believed that, barring any major flare-up in the interim, the warring factions in this dispute just might yet find some common ground and maybe get to settle their differences.

That and a hell of a lot more would depend on the next day's big meeting.

The miner paused on sighting the familiar ginger-thatched figure leaning against a lamp post.

'Hi there, Toby. Say, know where I can find Skelley?'

'How in hell should I know?'

The miner's face showed puzzlement in the sickly glow of the Federal Street lamplight.

'What's griping you, Toby? You and Skelley are best pards, that's why.'

'Don't never call him no pard of mine again, Red. I wouldn't spit on any *hombre* who'd sell us out.'

'You're talking about that meeting we got on tomorrow? Heck, I don't see that just talking to Wardlaw is selling anybody out.'

'Then you're just as blind and thick-witted as he is,' Toby John snarled, and flung away.

The angry little man kept on until reaching the far end of Federal Street where the old water pump stood. He halted and leaned upon it, glaring bleakly back at the lights. Right now, driven by his always lusty appetites, and still with a little cash money left, he knew he could be living it up at the gambling tables, fondling the girls and drinking himself stupid, or maybe even starting a big head-splitting brawl, were he in that mood.

But he wasn't.

These bleak days days he found he couldn't indulge himself or even think about anything other than 'The Struggle'. He figured things wouldn't and couldn't improve for him until this showdown with Wardlaw was settled, leastways.

For little Toby John was that rarest of all Western species – a rich man who still cared deeply for the class he'd left behind that day he'd struck the bright seams of butter-yellow gold and gleaming silver in far California.

Most of that fortune had already gone in support for the miners involved in the bitter strike which he'd found raging back here upon his return from the golden West.

Squinting and muttering he focused upon the twinkling lights atop Wardlaw Hill, envisioning Wardlaw and his slinky wife seated before a huge meal of duck and wine with their new killer looking on, most likely. While down here they were sipping gruel with the hope of a leaf of boiled cabbage to follow – if they were real lucky.

Gnawing on a knuckle and brushing back a tear, Toby John railed and fumed silently at the way things were shaping, particularly since Wardlaw had imported his high-priced enforcer.

Wardlaw had brought in such men in the past but all had failed to impose any real control over himself and his workers.

But right from first glance he'd sensed Coder was different. So it had proven. The gunman was yet to kill anyone but it seemed he didn't have to. He exuded authority and power and Toby had seen for himself how his arrival at a ruckus could cause his strikers to turn to water and go slinking off like naughty boys – not like wronged working men whose families were starving.

Now the big strike which he'd initiated was faltering badly and he knew the Cousin Jacks would shortly be forced to give in and go back down the mines for the same old money – if they were lucky.

It was intolerable. But what could be done?

A month earlier he might have come up with some splendid new stratagem that might have handed his beloved poor their victory. But while the strikers faltered, bitterness, defeat and rotgut whiskey had undermined his own strength alarmingly and now his brain had lost its former clarity and purpose. Only his resentment burned more strongly and fiercely than ever.

The dark decision seemed simply to leak into his fevered brain just as his runty figure shuffled down Shotgun Street then on past the courthouse. Halting before the building where the proposed meeting was to take place next day, he felt a sick excitement rise within him, and his lips began to move: *One man. . . . Forget everything else. . . . Remove Wardlaw then stand back and watch the miners led by men of enlightenment like myself sit down together with the new owners and calmly plan out every step of a bright and harmonious future together. . . .*

But surely Wardlaw would never submit while ever he was protected by that gun from Nogales?

Yet that was still only just one man. . . .

One man – one bullet?

It was like a moment of revelation and Toby was still smiling strangely upon entering Matt Dunstan's Wine Rooms a short time later to limp across to the bar.

'Hey, you look mighty pleased with yourself tonight, Toby,' greeted Dunstan from behind his bar. 'What'll it be tonight? Your regular sarsaparilla?'

'No, not tonight, Matt. Tonight I'll have a two-cent dark.'

'Going off the wagon, eh, Toby? What's the occasion? Celebrating something?'

'You might say that,' Toby said with a faraway look. 'Yeah, reckon you might call it a celebration. . . .'

CHAPTER 7

THE VIOLENT TIDE

Wardlaw descended from the lofted front gallery and made for the stables with a scowl. Ryan Coder stood in the mid-morning shade putting the finishing touches to saddling his horse. He glanced up at the sound of steps, nodded when he saw who it was then continued with what he was doing.

'What's this?' Wardlaw's tone was sharp. He'd just emerged from yet another confrontation with his wife. Seemed it was mostly all they did these days. Fight. This was an irritation, yet was far from the top of his list of preoccupations. Today's new rumor was that Ace Deagan had boosted his support for the strikers, which came right at a time when Wardlaw sensed the Cousin Jacks might at last be about ready to quit their fight and agree to a return to work for the same old pay and conditions.

He scowled as the gunfighter turned his head. 'Didn't you hear me, mister? I said—'

'I've never figured "what's this" rated an answer.'

Wardlaw flushed but bit back his retort. He regarded Coder as distant and borderline arrogant, and yet every day congratulated himself for hiring the gunman. For even though Sedalia might seem to be growing more unsettled and dangerous by the day, Wardlaw continued to feel secure, due almost entirely to his somber gunman.

'Very well,' he conceded. 'I'll rephrase. Just where do you think you're going?'

Coder inclined his head toward the town lying sprawled under hot sunlight below them. He bent to tighten the cinch strap.

'Goddamnit, man, I need y—' Wardlaw began but Coder spoke over him.

'You're planning to work up here until mid-afternoon which means you won't need me here at all. But I need to show the flag down there and we both know it. Just because the strikers haven't marched up here again, or tried to fire the stopes, doesn't mean they mightn't try something.'

'All right, damnit!' Wardlaw stepped back and gestured. 'Well, what are you waiting for? Go do what you have to.' An uncertain pause, then: 'But make sure you don't go taking any unnecessary risks, hear?'

Coder swung up.

'I never do. . . .'

His words trailed off. He was looking beyond Wardlaw. The man turned sharply to see his wife approaching along the gravel pathway. Rhea looked striking as always and Wardlaw's dark eyes glittered with both lust and aggravation.

Before either man could speak Rhea held up a warning finger to her husband.

'No . . . no more arguments.' She stopped to smile at the gunfighter, then tossed her silky hair and spread her arms. 'My, what a lovely morning for – well, for whatever is it you're planning to do today, Ryan?'

'Just my job.'

'My, Ryan sounds almost as grim as you are today, darling,' she said. 'It makes me wonder sometimes what it must be like to be a man with all those big nasty problems to be sorted out every day and—'

Her words ended as Coder turned his mount around to go loping away across the hill slope for the trail. Wardlaw called after him but he didn't respond. He had his reasons. The couple's stormy relationship irked him for reasons he wasn't sure of. But more important was the simple fact that he felt the need to get to town quickly and be seen making his regular rounds.

Today he wanted to 'show the flag' while maintaining a constant watch.

In general he felt satisfied with the situation in Sedalia at the moment even though aware things were far from stable. That brief period of quiet which had followed the mob's march upon the hill had deteriorated back into the old pattern of brawling between Regulators and strikers, plus the usual rumors of plots, sabotage and hell just around the corner.

The planned public meeting should help clear the air, he mused, as he left the last of the timber behind and made for the bridge across the stream. He didn't envision a quick settlement of the strike but would be satisfied with any progress.

He sighted strikers from the Motherlode and Sister Fan holding a sizable meeting on the vacant lot next to Connelly's woodyard when he walked by later.

Heads turned but nobody reacted. Maybe that was encouraging? Maybe. . . .

Back on the main stem he noticed several town-women making for the miners' quarter toting food and pots of coffee.

When he paused to nod approvingly he was unaware that he was in turn under sharp and hostile scrutiny from the upper gallery of the Red Wall Saloon where a flamboyant Ace Deagan was torching his first stogie of the day.

'You notice something?' the saloon-keeper remarked, flicking ash from his silk cravat. 'Every time they relieve him of nursemaiding Wardlaw up on the hill that gunshark makes straight for this quarter. It's like he's just watching and waiting for some-

99

one about my size to start raising hell. You jokers notice that too?'

The two bodyguards and a bartender simply shrugged. All were hard men and needed to be, working for Ace. But the truth was Coder intimidated even the gunhands, and that was enough to make everybody at the Red Wall edgy.

'Well, great bunch of high-class paid help I've got myself!' Deagan was sarcastic as he torched a stogie into life with a sweep of a lucifer. 'Like hell!' He sucked smoke deep into his lungs with gusto. Then, 'Honeychile, just what was it that Wardlaw's hot-shot *pistolero* said to you about me again?'

Honeychile stifled a yawn. She was usually sound asleep this time of day.

'I told you, Ace, he never said much of nothing. But he did ask a mess of questions about who works for you, what your plans are for the town – that sort of stuff. But I think you could be wrong about that feller. He struck me as kinda nice and—'

'Get back inside,' Deagan cut her off. 'I pay you to hustle shots, not to run off at the mouth.'

The girl left crestfallen. Straddling a chair, henchman Spade Hood serviced big white teeth with a matchstick. 'You know, she could be half-right about Coder, boss. Mebbe he ain't after your curly scalp like you seem to figure, after all?'

'You can bet he's after me.'

Deagan began pacing the floor. A man who'd worked his way up by both fair means and foul, he

100

was playing for the highest of high stakes these days. He'd laid out big money to finance the miners, his long-term plan being first to cripple Wardlaw financially then take over his mines.

King of Chad Valley!

He'd been watching his plans heading in that direction the day a brooding gunfighter showed up out of nowhere to threaten everything virtually overnight. . . .

The outcome of that development was that Wardlaw was still standing strong against the strikers while Ace Deagan was drinking too much rye and losing power and money by the day – all because of that big gun from Nogales!

Worse, he felt he was threatening to come apart lately, was still unable to figure out how to erase the Coder problem without personal risk for Ace Deagan.

'Wardlaw keeps claiming he hired that gun just to protect him from the strikers,' he brooded out loud. 'But it sure looks to me Coder's cozying up with some of those Cousin Jacks, instead of kicking ass. And that in turn tells me louder every day he must've signed on either to run me out or put me under the ground. Nothing else makes sense, so nobody try and tell me it does.'

It never paid to argue with Ace Deagan, so nobody tried. Instead everybody got serious and got busy conjuring up the names of gunmen Deagan might recruit if he was really serious about eliminating the Coder threat.

101

Until one of his audience had heard enough.

'Look, if you'd just let me get me bloomin' mitts on him, Ace, it'd be all over while you were thinkin' about it,' Limehouse Jack rumbled from his great barrel of a chest. He fingered his scarred brow where Coder had caught him with his gun butt.

'Oh, yeah – just half a minute would do. 'Is little tin gun won't do him much bloody good once I hook these mitts on him. You can believe that if you never believe nothin' else.'

Deagan studied the giant pensively. He didn't doubt Limehouse could back up his brag, given half a chance. But surely any kind of chance was unlikely? Ryan Coder was a gunman and not a brawler. They did their work with Colts, not fists, a fact of life he now reiterated to Limehouse.

But the giant remained unimpressed with his reasoning.

'Look, boss, this Coder's prideful, a blind man can see that. He looks married to that big Colt of his, but knows he could never shoot me down on account I don't pack no gun. But if I was to pick the right moment I'll wager I could taunt him to takin' me on just out of pride.' He paused and spread huge hands. 'And the minute he done that it'd be all over for Wardlaw's bleedin' bodyguard and you'd be top of the heap, Ace. Can't you see it?'

'No . . . crazy!' Deagan muttered after a moment of pacing to and fro. Then he stopped and massaged his jaw, thinking. Or was it crazy? There'd already been bad blood between Limey and Coder. Surely the giant had the right to demand satisfaction with weapons of his own choosing – as any man should?

At last he nodded. He found the notion encouraging if still not entirely persuasive. But surely it was a chance?

He said, 'All right, maybe I'll think it over. But don't be going off half-cocked. The Cousin Jacks are planning a big meeting tomorrow and they've never been more desperate. Maybe if we can fire them up and pour enough free booze into them they might run amok and roll right over Wardlaw anyway, in which case I wouldn't have to worry about his lousy gunpacker.'

'OK, boss, we'll do it your way.' Limehouse held out a huge hand. 'But if things don't pan out that way—' His clenched fist smacked into his palm with a report like a gunshot.

'If that's the case, then he's all yours.'

'Mine!' breathed Limehouse Jack, and pumped the air with mighty fists, the hero of battles already won.

Rhea Wardlaw was sipping wine and idly watching her husband in the sunlit courtyard below as he held a hostler by his bandanna with one hand while repeatedly striking him in the face with the other.

The woman's face was expressionless as she drained the last of the wine and turned for the liquor cabinet.

She halted.

Coe Neeley stood silhouetted in the doorway.

'Well?' she said brusquely, 'what is it now?'

The man crossed to her quickly and made to take her in his arms. She brushed him aside and reached for the bottle.

'It's true, isn't it, Rhea?'

'What? That if it doesn't rain the creeks won't rise?' She smiled and raised her glass in a mocking gesture. 'To you, Coe – last of the great romantics!'

And drank deep.

'Why, Rhea?' he said. 'Why Coder – of all people? Why couldn't you throw me over for someone at least halfway decent? That butcher is just a—'

'Why did I break it off with us?' she cut in. 'Because I woke up one day this week realizing I'd just met someone who, whatever his faults, is a real man. There, is everything plain now, my little love-pet?'

'You're drunk, Rhea.'

'But I'll be sober tomorrow, while you'll still be the frightened little money-counter who—'

She broke off as footsteps sounded on the stairs. She held up her glass and laughed tauntingly. 'Heavy steps, Coe. Could be either my husband or the man I might take as a lover. Both of them more than a little scary, so hadn't you better vanish, darling?'

The mines manager disappeared and for moments all was quiet in the perfume-scented room before Coder appeared in the doorway.

'Rhea.' His voice was deep. 'Where's Wardlaw?'

'Where indeed?' she smiled, coming towards him. 'Could be in the library or, who knows? He could even be creeping up the stairs in the hope of catching us together—'

She broke off at the sound of heavy doors opening, followed by an imperious shout from the lobby. With a teasing giggle she reached for him, but Coder was already on his way out.

'He'll be angry if he sees you drunk,' he warned, making for the stairs.

In that instant she was almost sober; maybe she'd only been faking anyway. Quickly she followed him out on to the landing with tears in her eyes.

'Please . . . I was drinking just to give myself the courage to beg you to help me.' She extended a shaking hand as he paused uncertainly at the top of the stairs. She was a little drunk, yet needed to be. 'I must escape but nobody will help me. They're all too afraid of my husband. But you aren't afraid, Ryan. You don't fear anybody. Please—?'

His brow knotted in puzzlement. For a moment he was struck both by how beautiful and how unhappy she looked. Then he heard movement below, muttered, 'Better sleep it off,' and descended the stairs two at a time.

'What about how angry I'll be if you don't admit you love me?' she taunted. 'Oh, do say you love me, Ryan. Just once? I so need someone to love me. . . .'

Coder's face remained blank as he reached the

ground floor. He'd not seen the beautiful mistress of Wardlaw Hill drunk before yet was hardly surprised. Their marriage was a farce if he was any judge.

Then he reassured himself. Maybe it was just a cliché – lovely bored wife and hard-driving husband under heavy pressure. Nothing new there. And surely no business of his anyway.

Or was it?

That thought took him unawares and caused him to pause, looking back up. But characteristically he shook his head and reminded himself of just who, what and where he was.

There was danger in the air and, as always, the safety of the man who paid his way must come first – and he was sure he'd sensed something threatening building up upon the streets of the town right now.

He couldn't let Wardlaw down even if he was a son of a bitch.

'Well, what's the latest from the war zone?' Wardlaw greeted sardonically as he entered the huge room where windows were opened to a gentle afternoon breeze. 'Or can I guess? The miners have joined forces with Ace Deagan and they plan to march on us en masse at midnight and burn us to the ground?'

Coder took out tobacco and papers. He stood relaxed with his weight on one leg in the shafting bars of light.

The Wardlaws were difficult people to understand but this was the first time he'd had both of them perhaps coming apart and seeming to act out of character at the same time.

Maybe this was untimely yet hardly surprising. Too rich, too spoiled and too out of love – that was his diagnosis. And yet again warned himself that none of that was any concern of his. He had just two preoccupations right now: Wardlaw's safety and whatever was building up down in the town.

Instinct convinced the man of the gun that events were moving towards a climax in Sedalia. The town was alive with rumors and uncertainty, punctuated by sudden eruptions of violence. Up until today he'd felt his presence on the streets had exerted a calming effect, but this was no longer the case.

The hold-out strikers were starving and fighting amongst themselves when not starting street brawls with anybody from Wardlaw Hill. The town itself was suddenly being torn apart by rivalries, factions, suspicion and violence at an ever increasing pace, and it was high time the only person who might be able to rein it all in and come up with a solution was the one standing before him drinking his whiskey neat.

He wouldn't pull his punches, he decided as he took out his stogies and felt his pockets for vestas before getting started.

But when he was through the big man simply shrugged. He set his untasted drink aside and hooked hands into his lapels and looked Coder straight in the eye.

'You could be right, gunfighter, for I smelt something down there today but didn't want to face up to it. But plainly we can't buck reality. We've got mobs roaming the streets and the saloons filled to overflowing with drunks and malcontents. Meanwhile, Skelley is pulling his hair out in frustration and Toby John is all over the damned town like a disease trying to whip the Cousin Jacks up into staging another march on us. Latest I hear is that bastard Deagan is pulling strings behind the scenes and hatching up fresh mischief. So . . . is that about how we both see things, or maybe there is more?'

Coder glanced at the whiskey bottle. He hesitated, then crossed to the sideboard and poured himself a half shot. He downed it at a gulp. The good warmth lifted him, and yet he knew he would not take another until whatever was building up was either resolved or had exploded onto the streets.

An odd calm semed to envelop both men when they settled down to review the changing situation. One by one they identified the potential trouble spots and considered their resources which comprised Wardlaw's Regulators and the ranch-hands, should the worst happen.

And Coder and his big black gun.

Deliberately calm, Coder stated his belief that it might be possible to keep the lid on the town overnight. If so, he wouldn't be surprised to see whatever malevolent bug of rebellion which had infected Sedalia eventually expire from simple exhaustion, as he'd seen happen in other towns at other times.

But behind his hard gunfighter's face, he was thinking: *Maybe if you just offered these poor bastards something – anything – they might just call off the strike and return to work, for God knows they're not asking much.*

But the words were never spoken. Once before he'd raised the miners' claims and come up against a stone wall. A yawning gap separated miner from mine boss and never the two should meet, so it seemed. And why should that bother him? He was a gunfighter and as such had no business meddling in such abstracts as right or wrong.

'So, at this point,' he summarized, 'the best thing we can do is go show ourselves on the streets. Let them see we're not afraid and are ready for anything they might throw up. That might look like bluff but I've had it work for me more than once.

He paused. 'I'll go put it to them. I want you to stay put here, Mr Wardlaw—'

'We'll go together,' came the quick response, and Coder was not surprised. Wardlaw might be an arrogant bastard but plainly cowardice was not amongst his shortcomings.

'So, what are we waiting for?' he murmured, and they left the mansion together to stride for the stables.

Had they glanced up they might have seen Rhea's pale face staring down from the parapets. The liquor had worn off and tears shimmered in her eyes as her lips moved silently. She was praying for the quickly receding riders, for herself, and for Sedalia.

The fiery runt whom the miners regarded as their spokesman and champion, stood in the shadows directly across from the looming bulk of the council chambers where next day's proposed meeting was scheduled.

It would be Glede Skelley versus mine boss Wardlaw. Again.

Having taken part in the preceding failed meetings Toby John had vowed never to be part of that sham again.

He knew it would all come to nothing. A cynical exercise intended merely to appease the anger of his starving Cousin Jacks a little longer until they would reach the brink of starvation and be forced to throw in their hand.

That would mean a return to work for no gain and the whole cycle would begin again. Miner overworked and underpaid – miner boss growing richer every day.

As it had been before when he'd headed West to search for gold, and found it.

In this uneasy night it was all too easy to recall the zest and enthusiasm with which he'd returned triumphant to Sedalia with his sack of yellow gold and his dreams of finally setting the miners free of their shackles to recover their manhood and dignity as owner-workers, with everything that would entail.

A tear filled his eye. What a dreamer he'd been! A

blind, trusting fool! Things had never worked that way and never would, as he knew only too well by now. The mine bosses were far too clever and ruthless for the Toby Johns of the West. He'd had that proven to him until now he was just as poor as the poorest once again – with nothing left but a shattered dream, a raging sense of injustice, and the hate.

CHAPTER 8

BROKEN TRUST

A hairy-faced miner in ragged denim paused upon sighting the hunched figure propping up a lamp post.

'Hey, Toby. Where can I find Skelley?'

'How the hell would I know?'

The miner looked puzzled. 'What's griping you, Toby? I always figured you and Glede were the best of pards.'

'Pards? I wouldn't spit on a man who'd sell his own out.'

'You mean this meeting with Wardlaw? Hell, I don't see that simply sitting down and talking with the man shapes up as selling anybody out. We all—'

'Then you're an even bigger fool than Skelley!' John snarled and flung away.

The fierce little man stumped off to the far end of Federal Street, to the old water pump there. Leaning

112

upon it he gazed bleakly up at the lighted house atop Wardlaw Hill and envisioned the copper king and that slinky wife of his seating to a huge supper with their two-bit killer. While down here poor folks were sipping thin gruel with the eternal stale stink of old cabbage drifting over their sorry rooftops.

Too bad that hardcase he'd hired a month ago to kill Wardlaw had not proven up to the job. . . .

Nobody knew about that. It had been his plan entirely. Hire a badman to kill Wardlaw. Sounded simple, but wasn't. The attempt had failed, and simply thinking about it caused him suddenly to stiffen, feeling again that odd sensation as if his brain was overheating when that old lethal impulse returned to take firm hold.

The last bum he'd secretly hired to kill Wardlaw had looked and acted like a genuine gunshark until that thug Wardlaw had stabbed him to death. But one triumph had certainly not rendered Wardlaw invincible, he reassured himself, swabbing a feverish brow now. With another big assembly meeting imminent tonight, how could just one lone gun wolf such as Coder smell out a single determined man in a crowd the size of the one expected at the courthouse within the hour?

He was aware he was sweating profusely and his hands were shaking. Yet he stayed focused, reassuring himself no man could watch everybody, particularly a sawn-off little runt like himself who was as familiar upon these streets as the stink of cooked cabbage from Nelson's Diner!

Although a man who rarely smiled, his mounting sense of outrage against Wardlaw perversely saw him wearing a strange secret smile as he entered Dunstan's Wine Rooms a short time later to limp across to the bar.

'Hey, you're looking mighty pleased with yourself tonight, Toby,' Dunstan remarked. 'What'll it be? Sarsaparilla?'

'Not tonight, Matt. Give me a two-cent dark.'

'So, going off the wagon again, eh, Toby? What's the occasion? Celebrating something?'

'You could say that,' little Toby said with a strange faraway look. 'Yeah, I guess you might call it celebrating . . . in advance. . . .'

A cooler breeze was rising that narrow twilight as two horsemen swung into sight around the corner of the Sedalia Fast Freight. The wind caught the dust raised by a passing freighter and blew it in gusts towards the ragged mob of silent citizens assembled before the courthouse.

The cross wind fluttered the tattered flag atop the big frame building and set to creaking the sign that said Law Office outside the window where turnkey Cal Rogers sat trembling nervously, sensing the strange tension. For though it was early evening and still hot there seemed to be almost a hint of a chill in the breeze that snaked up along Shotgun Street from the valley.

'I don't like it,' growled Wardlaw as his mount rolled its eyes back at him. 'There's something in the air – and it's all too damned quiet.'

'Just another day,' reassured Coder, raking both sides of the darkening street with a gimlet eye.

His companion muttered and adjusted the set of his hat. Wardlaw was puzzled, a rare state of mind for him. For even though sure of yet another victory over the rabble tonight he was unusually tense and kept glancing at Coder as if for reassurance.

The gunfighter's silent presence provided it. Dressed in sober broadcloth with flat-brimmed black hat shading a face that was all hard planes and angles, Coder was assurance itself as they clattered on by the knot of sullen figures in miners' rags lounging before the city billiard parlor, without eliciting even a catcall.

Reassured, Wardlaw sat up a little straighter in the saddle as they approached the Red Wall Saloon, where a booming voice suddenly shattered the unnatural quiet.

'Who's yer friend, Wardlaw? Surely it ain't that terrible fierce gunman from Nogales?'

Coder glanced up to sight the unmistakable figure of Limehouse Jack looming above a bunch of saloon loafers.

'Oh, holy mother, the terrible bad gunman is lookin' straight at me now,' the man howled in mock terror. 'Mercy, mother, mercy!'

Somebody sniggered while others scuttled away

from the giant as though fearing his taunting might draw a violent response from the gunman. Who could be sure how the Coder breed reacted to anything?

But the gunfighter just rode on by, leaving the giant Englishman glaring after them with pendulous jaw sagging in disappointment.

'Are you going to let him get away with that?' Wardlaw muttered.

'He's not getting away with anything,' came Coder's quiet reply. 'He just thinks he is.'

The two continued on without further incident to approach the courthouse where a hundred miners were assembled, waiting. To Coder's experienced eye and ear the mood of the mob seemed about right and he sensed the workers might have decided to set their former violence at such gatherings aside and maybe try for common sense and discussion, for a big change.

It was in that very instant that he glimpsed the gun!

Toby John was almost invisible in back of the nearest bunch of strikers grouped around a stack of hay bales piled before the livery stables adjacent to the courthouse. Amongst that sea of dour yet almost hopeful faces, Toby John's twisted little face was almost hidden beneath his wild shock of red hair which stood out like a flashing alarm beacon.

The little gun glinting in the man's hand was trained squarely upon Foley Wardlaw.

Coder's draw was instinctive. There was not one shaved sliver of a second for anything but response. If he didn't act faster than he'd ever done before then the man he was pledged to protect was dead.

His Colt filled his hand and crashed, its deep-throated voice obliterating the lighter metallic spang of John's weapon. Struck hard, the fierce litle figure lurched drunkenly as his misdirected bullet caught a ragged miner close by, spinning him about. An ashen-faced John somehow regained his balance and was struggling to line Wardlaw up in his sights again when Coder shot him through the heart.

A moment of total silence was followed by a roar of rage as Coder sprang from his saddle to face Glede Skelley as the man came rushing down the court-house steps.

'I had no choice, Skelley!' he shouted. 'He was shooting at Wardlaw and—'

A rock hissed from the crowd and caught his shoulder, causing him to lurch and drop his smoking gun. He dived for the weapon as the angry shouts of the miners became the blood-curdling bellow of the mob.

They closed in from all sides. Few had seen Toby John's gun. All the mob knew was that the gunfighter had shot down the little man who'd saved countless families from starvation over recent months .

They were wild with rage but Coder refused to back up so much as one step. 'Don't be loco!' he shouted in their faces. 'He tried to gun Wardlaw

117

down, damn you!'

'Butcher!' raged a black-bearded heavyweight, and Coder was sent spinning as a fist grazed the side of his head.

Tasting blood, he bobbed low under the next wild swing then rose to full height and belted the butt of his .45 into a snarling mouth, smashing teeth and spraying crimson. Hands like claws were clutching for him on all sides. He dived nimbly beneath his rearing horse and a man seized him by the leg. Coder whipped up a knee that caught him in the jaw and knocked him senseless.

He heard Wardlaw's cry of alarm. Instantly, Coder whirled away from his horse and ploughed through the surging press of bodies, breaking a man's arm with a downward chop from his revolver. Two angry miners were attempting to haul Wardlaw from his saddle while a third jabbed up at him with vicious thrusts of a tent pole.

Coder's Colt stormed again and the man wielding the pole reeled sideways clutching a bloodied shoulder. Another fast shot and the grimed figure who had hold of Wardlaw's boot howled and grabbed his thigh before toppling into the dust.

'Get on back to the house!' Coder roared at Wardlaw. Then ducked low beneath a desperate dive by a ginger-headed miner who slammed head-first into an upright then toppled slowly backwards, out to the world.

He had a glimpse of Wardlaw spurring his mount

viciously to burst his way through the surging ranks of grey and dirty white. Next instant somebody kicked him in the guts with brutal force. He reeled backwards and triggered at point-blank range. The shot took the miner below the knee, the flash of gunpowder setting fire to his dungarees as he howled and fell, writhing in agony.

The fight which had begun close by the court-house had by this surged halfway across Shotgun Street, with far fewer miners menacing Coder now as citizens came running to intervene from all sides.

There was no telling how long the chaos might have lasted but for Glede Skelley.

Amongst the first to get to Coder after John fell, a raging Skelley had been instantly belted off his feet by one of Coder's powerhouse swings. The man lay sprawled and helpless almost a minute before struggling to his knees.

He blinked, shook his head, stared wide-eyed.

Toby John lay dead on his back mere feet away and Skelley slowly realized he was staring dumbly at a wicked little derringer clutched in the dead man's right hand. The revelation struck like a bullet.

Coder had gunned Toby down in defense of both himself and the man he rode for!

Lurching to his feet with blood trickling from his mouth, Skelley staggered after the mob which now had Coder backed up against the wall of the Greasy Thumb Café. The gunfighter's hat was gone and his gun was empty yet he appeared to be defending with even greater ferocity than before.

'He had a gun, boys!' he shouted at the top of his lungs. 'Toby had a gun in his hand!'

Coder ducked beneath a haymaker and smashed his elbow into a stubbled jaw. 'He was about to cut Wardlaw down!' he affirmed, kicking an attacker's legs out from under him before quickly reloading his six-gun.

Shouts of 'No!' and 'Murderer!' rose from the mob. But even as some continued to rage others were running across to where John had fallen to see for themselves.

The unfired weapon still lay clutched in a dead hand for every man to see – and frenzied mob fury was already starting to recede even before a cowboy held the dead man's arm high for all to see the limp hand clutching the vicious little two-shot.

'It's been fired!' he shouted. 'And his finger is still on the trigger! See for yourselves!'

Brawlers sagged in sudden exhaustion against one another while others simply stopped slugging, and shook their heads. With their rage ebbing and soon gone they stared about in a daze to realize just how many injured were sprawled about in the dust, while others wandered about bleeding and confused.

'I had no choice but to shoot !' Coder yelled in the heavy hush. He swung accusingly upon a pale Glede Skelley. 'He tried to murder Wardlaw – and you had to know it, by God!'

Skelley shook his head like a weary old man. 'I

didn't know anything about it, man. Whatever Toby did, he done on his own.'

'Yeah, well he did plenty,' Coder said bitterly. He stepped away into the quietening street, raised his voice. 'I believe Wardlaw might have at last been ready to meet you strikers halfway today before this. But he's already on his way home now and I doubt if you'll ever get him to sit down and parley again!'

You could almost hear the quiet as he dropped his arms and turned away.

The street was still crowded some time later when Coder located his horse and swung into the saddle. He stared straight ahead and said not another word as he rode slowly off like a man who'd aged years in as many minutes.

It was moments later that the slender figure ran from the crowd before the bank to reach up and seize his horse by the bridle bit.

'Come on, Mr Coder,' Honeychile said. 'You need a drink if ever a feller did.'

He realized he didn't have the strength to argue. He wordlessly swung the horse's head and followed the girl away through the thinning crowds.

He was coming out of it by the time they reached broad Crow Street where a cooling breeze from the east breathed fresh life into him and he felt the exhaustion from battle-weary legs and arms begin to ease.

I've jousted with Death again . . . and won, he thought as, with head tilted back, he allowed her to guide him onwards along the back streets in the direction of Clancy's Bar. Before they reached their objective he felt a sudden return of power surge through his body anew. He looked up and the stars seemed to hang so close he felt he could almost touch them with his tongue.

Coe Neeley threw a double brandy down his throat before stepping out upon the saloon's top gallery to watch the sun struggle free of the hills.

A thin cloud of dust ghosted the town far below, forcing Wardlaw's man to shade his eyes with his hand while he squinted along the broad strip of Main Street. He eventually made out the squad of shabby figures in ragged miners' grey marching and holding a tattered banner aloft.

'Morons,' he sneered, then turned sharply at the sound of a footfall. Foley Wardlaw emerged fully dressed with a cigar clenched between his teeth.

'Down there, Mr Wardlaw! Look at those idiots. Don't they ever learn—'

He broke off with a hiccup and Wardlaw's gaze turned icy.

'Drinking at this hour, mister? Again?'

Neeley swayed slightly. It had been a long night. He realized he was drunk but seemed no longer to care.

'Maybe you should join me, boss,' he half grinned. 'After all, I believe we're both of us losers this morning.'

'What the hell are you talking about?'

'Why, love and loss, of course. That sound interesting, Mr Wardlaw?' Neeley spread his hands wide. 'Well, your wife has a new hero today after what happened last night, and so have you. And, would you believe, both your heroes are the same man? Your gunfighter! Welcomed him home here at the mansion like a gladiator, so she did. And I could have been just a fly on the wall – instead of the man who really loves her.'

Wardlaw crossed to the man and backhanded him across the face, felling him to the floor.

'What drivel are you talking, Neeley? Are you saying—?'

'I'm saying I love your wife but she loves Coder. Could anything be plainer than that—?' Neeley broke off to dab at his bloodied mouth, appearing to sober a little. 'Don't believe me, huh? Why not go take a look at them in there at breakfast, then tell me what I say isn't so.'

He broke off. He was talking to himself. By the time he'd recovered his flask to take another badly needed slug, his employer was standing unnoticed in the dining room archway sixty feet distant watching his wife and Ryan Coder – together.

What Wardlaw saw he found vaguely disturbing, although nothing like Neeley had implied. His wife stood behind the gunfighter's chair with her hands on his shoulders, her head bent forward and golden hair tumbling, whispering something he could not catch. A little over-familiar, maybe, but surely nothing more.

Then he heard the gunfighter's quiet response: 'Better take your chair before Mr Wardlaw shows, Rhea. He mightn't understand.'

'Not understand what?' the woman said distinctly. 'That I'm tired of pretending with him . . . of being afraid of him? What's not to understand?'

'Good question!'

Wardlaw's words caused the woman to move away from the gunfighter and occupy her own chair before he reached the table. For a long moment Wardlaw stood staring from one to the other, fighting back suspicion.

Without looking up, Coder used a silver fork to spear a corn fritter. He bit into it and chewed, a picture of relaxed detachment.

Wardlaw appeared to deflate. One, he owed this man his life following last night. Two, this was an old game his wife was playing. He treated her very badly in private and sometimes in public she attempted to strike back.

And yet – had he seen something in her eyes before he'd interrupted? Something that might have been far more than mere flirting?

The answer was a resounding *yes*. Instantly rage and jealousy struck deep but were not permitted to show.

In that moment he hated both his wife and the man who'd just saved his life, knew himself well enough to know he would punish them both.

But not now.

Only his pride and vanity were threatened in this moment of revelation. Bigger stakes were in play. He'd come within a hair's breadth of being murdered that night, and the power game he played was still far from over. He would still bring the strikers to their knees and see them back at work on his terms before he would even start thinking about revenge.

Yet he found he still couldn't speak for fear of giving himself away. He went to the liquor cabinet and poured himself a stiff shot, his wife watching him warily while Coder watched her.

Coder's expression didn't change. Outwardly he still looked the hard man of the gun, solid, dangerous but relaxed. Inside was like another country, for in the space of mere minutes he'd come to recognize and understand the mixed emotions he'd experienced in the wake of the riot.

He'd felt death whisper close – again – and in the emotional aftermath had seen Rhea Wardlaw with new eyes and realized what he'd thought of as his mere liking for Rhea was something infinitely stronger.

And he had thought: *Gunfighter, you've finally broken your own rule. Never get involved on a gun job.*

He rose abruptly from the table. She looked so lovely and suddenly fearful that for a moment he wanted to tell her of his feelings, somehow assure her all would be well – and that he'd protect her and even take her away where she would be safe and loved.

He did none of those things, simply collected his hat and fitted it to his head carefully as though its placement was of great importance.

For his word was his bond and the habits of a lifetime guaranteed his commitment to guard and protect the man he was contracted to.

He could only hope she would understand.

'Watch your back when I'm gone,' was his last advice to Foley Wardlaw. And 'Adios' was all he had for beautiful Rhea.

The woman cried out and rushed after him as he quit the room. She was calling his name when Neeley reappeared to restrain her then closed the big doors.

Coder was conscious of many eyes watching from the great house when he rode out to take the downhill trail until he was lost from the sight of the mansion watchers in the dust and smoke of the town.

His emotions were in check and he was thinking with cool clarity as he swung into the broad main street, where nothing appeared to be as it had been before.

He expected that.

For a man had died and many injured earlier, and such events always created their own aftermath. With blood spilled and old rivalries and hatreds exposed, it would be some time before Sedalia could call itself normal again.

In the meantime he had plenty thinking to do.

Main Street widened before him as he pointed the horse towards the White Dime Eatery where an opened window emitted fragrant cooking scents upon the early morning air.

The good honest smell of steak with southern fried onions greeted him as he walked inside and took off his hat.

He saw her the moment she appeared in the doorway with Neeley at her elbow, felt a tingling in his wrists as he saw how lovely yet fearful she appeared in this smoky light.

He was standing by the time the couple reached him, the first thing he noticed the dark bruising down one side of her face.

'Oh, I'm so relieved you're all right,' Rhea gasped, taking him by the arms. 'After you'd gone I had the terrible feeling that the miners might – you are all right aren't you, Ryan?'

He nodded as he held her, shooting a questioning glance at Wardlaw's deputy.

'I tried to get Mrs Wardlaw to stay put.' Neeley seemed to have sobered in the past two hours. He shrugged. 'But after what happened . . . well. . . .'

'What happened?' Coder repeated, eyes on that dark mark. 'Did Ward—?'

'That doesn't matter,' the woman cut him off. She held his arms tightly. 'But I'm only sorry that he made me so angry – and I said what I said.'

The eyes of the eatery were upon them. Coder drew

127

the woman down to a chair then sat facing her. It seemed something powerful was connecting them, and it was not the first time he'd experienced that sensation when they'd been together. Of course he'd brushed it aside each time, for when he signed on to protect someone that man could rely upon his total loyalty.

But he'd never encountered a Rhea Wardlaw before: that had been plain from the day he'd first ridden through the huge gates up there on Wardlaw Hill.

'Rhea—' he began uncertainly, but she cut him off, stealing a quick glance at the doors.

'No time, Ryan.' She squeezed his hand and met his eyes. 'Please, now that my husband has the foolish notion there is something between us, I have no idea what he may do. He needs you and depends on you, but even that mightn't prevent him doing something to harm you. You must give me your word you'll leave right now, tonight. I want you to go and not come back, for if anything happened to you I wouldn't want to live. . . .'

There was more, even though the gunfighter was shaking his head. No. He couldn't leave, not now when he realized she might be in danger. But it wasn't until they were on their way back to Wardlaw Hill, where they found Wardlaw had fallen into a drunken sleep, that he understood his reasons for staying went far deeper.

CHAPTER 9

SHOWDOWN

'When you're ready, Carl!'

'You don't honestly figure you can shade me, do you, Holly?'

Standing in the slanting rays of a blood-red sundown upon the crooked main street of Ruby Flats, Holly smiled across at the guntoter leaning against an upright sixty feet away.

'I don't just figure – I know it, Rogan.'

Carl Rogan, a sinister young man with ten honest notches hacked into his gun handle, suddenly switched from mocking to deeply curious.

'What's really goin' on here, Holly? Somebody hire you to come after me? I figure that's gotta be it. I mean, Bill Hickok hisself wouldn't brace me just to prove a point. So with you, it's got to be money!'

'The why of it doesn't make any difference, Rogan. Whether I'm putting you down for dollars or just for the hell of it, you'll wind up dead either way. But, like my ol' man always said, enough talk. Let's get on with it.'

Once more, lethal Rogan smiled. But it didn't hold as he realized the gunman from Nogales was deadly serious. But it still didn't make sense. For he'd never come close to losing a gun duel, and Holly knew it. So why would the Nogales gun risk getting blown to hell – for no good reason?

Yet puzzled one moment, Rogan was abruptly ice-cold and supremely confident the next. He'd cut his eye teeth on gun punks like this, and without an instant's hesitation launched into the smoothest and fastest draw Holly had ever faced.

It wasn't fast enough.

Too swift for the eye to follow, Holly came clear and two rapid-fire shots slammed brutally into his adversary's body and felled him in an instant as though struck by a giant's fist.

Wreathed in gunsmoke, Holly was smiling as he watched Rogan somehow fight his way up to a kneeling position. The man tried to raise his unfired piece but now it weighed a ton.

The crash of Holly's final shot seemed to fill his world and carried him into eternity.

In the echoing silence that followed, Holly was barely aware of gaping onlookers. All that signified for the young gun was that he'd just reaffirmed his invincibility. He'd needed final proof of that before continuing on for his date with destiny.

In Sedalia.

Midnight.

The servants had brought wine and whiskey to the glittering dining room but no food had been called for as yet.

Rhea Wardlaw sat sipping delicately from a crystal cut-glass but there was nothing delicate about the way her husband was putting away the imported brandy.

Wardlaw was celebrating his escape from death mere hours earlier. Yet even more exhilarating was the news that had just arrived from the town.

Down there, a hastily convened meeting of striking miners had resulted in a decision to return to work immediately, in light of the night's events. At this very moment his company Regulators were busy down there in the sickly yellow light of the Motherlode and Sister Fan, unlocking the gates and supervizing preparations for the first shift due to start work at 7 a.m. Sharp.

'Just to think I was prepared to maintain the lock-out for another month before importing strike-breakers,' Wardlaw repeated with a self-satisfied smile. 'When all it took to turn them to water was for that runt to try and murder me and Ryan to finish him off—'

'Foley,' Rhea interrupted from across the table, 'I believe you've already gloated enough, don't you agree? Do you think we might get to eat before I

131

drink myself under the table?'

Wardlaw flushed and seemed about to retort before remembering this was a celebration.

'To you, my ever-impeccably correct wife!' he replied, hoisting his glass. He clapped his hands and called, 'Entrées!'

The servants waiting in the anteroom emerged quickly and silently to place the elegant entrée dishes before each diner with the exception of Coder.

The gunman waved his serving aside as he subsequently did with each of the various courses. At last Coe Neeley was curious enough to remark, 'Surely you can't still be feeling badly about events, Coder? I mean, gunplay is your trade after all, is it not?'

Coder glanced at the man but made no response. He still felt numbed by the gunplay yet tried to believe he had no regrets. He'd saved Wardlaw's life and that was simply what he was hired to do.

'Sorry – maybe I've stepped on your gentleman's toes, Rhea—' Neeley slurred, but fell silent at a warning glare from Rhea Wardlaw and fumblingly picked up his glass.

'They'll all get over it.' Wardlaw sounded sure. 'And everyone just remember, this entire messy affair was of their own doing from start to finish. It was the Cousin Jacks who called the strike and I merely moved in as was my right to lock them out until they came to their senses, and to protect the mines against vandalism.'

He rose briskly and began pacing around the overladen mahogany table.

'Bloodshed was always inevitable since they first went on strike, and Deagan started lending them aid and comfort in the hope that in time I'd cave in. Well, I've whipped them all, that conniving Deagan as well. The pit whistles are going to sound in just a few hours and we can congratulate ourselves that Sedalia is now a far better and safer place without strikers or scum fanatics like Toby John around.'

He hefted his glass and his eyes swept challeng-ingly around the table.

'To the future!' he toasted, and everybody drank, including the gunfighter. None knew Coder was drinking to the repose of little Toby John's immortal soul.

There they went, tramping stolidly by below his high veranda of the Red Wall Saloon with knapsacks strapped to their backs and worn-out boots raising a steady drumming beat. After bitter weeks of strike and shut-down, the miners of Sedalia were once more to be seen heading for the shafts before the sun had cleared the rim.

Here and there an early riser cheered or a Deagan-hater jeered in triumph. But up where Ace Deagan stood chewing an unlit cheroot with arms folded tightly across his chest there was nothing but silence mingled with bitterness. He'd never expected the miners to knuckle under and call quits, as had finally occurred last night. This came as a body blow in view of his support of the hold-out. Over several long weeks the saloon-keeper had all but bankrupted himself assisting the miners to stay on strike with on-going handouts and food parcels while waiting for Wardlaw to go bust.

He'd been motivated entirely by self-interest, not generosity. His plan was to help the strikers hold out until Wardlaw went broke, then move in and snap up both mines for a song, get them working again, and fix his sights on building his first million – as a copper king.

So much for the best-laid plans, destroyed because one crazed cracker had pulled a gun on Wardlaw and got killed for his trouble. He'd seen the Cousin Jacks' defiance collapse within a matter of hours and their unanimous decision to go back underground had left Wardlaw up there on his high hill to pop the corks and start in celebrating his triumph. The big man had vowed to outlast the diggers, and had done it.

It was Ace Deagan's darkest hour and there wasn't a hint of his flashy style to be seen as he bit the cork out of a fresh bottle and drank deep.

But one thing was certain. He might be down tonight but tough Deagan was still far from out.

Three days passed almost without incident, and even the funeral of Toby John passed without disturbance.

Leaders such as Glede Skelley insisted that blame for the death of the little man being laid to rest belonged on John's own shoulders. It was that attitude from their leaders that kept the miners subdued and at peace – for now.

They were testing days for Glede Skelley. Yet he filled the vacant leadership smoothly enough and right away began building bridges between towners and Cousin Jacks, with an eye to the town's peaceful future.

The mood was far less congenial in Ace Deagan's empire of vice, dice and girls as he drank down the moon and watched Wardlaw go spanking past in his fine carriage with that blonde wife of his whom Ace had seriously planned to pursue and bed after he'd buried her husband and taken over the mines. So much for ambition and big plans!

It now looked as if he'd be lucky if he was simply able to hang onto his saloon, for one of Wardlaw's first moves after the Jacks knuckled under was to impose a total ban on the Red Wall Saloon for every digger who expected to keep his job.

By contrast this was the best of times for the self-styled King of Chad Valley. Yet although riding tall and never more visible on the streets with his high-priced gunman and Regulators in attendance, Wardlaw wasn't as secure as he might appear, and first to suspect this was his bodyguard.

Coder put in double hours during that time, and welcomed it. The shooting incident had hit him hard, so he preferred to be busy rather than brooding on the matter.

Several times in that period he'd come face to face with Limehouse Jack. The giant showed no fear and missed no opportunity to taunt him for 'killing midgets', yet Coder would not be goaded.

He had weightier concerns on his mind, such as his deepening interest in his employer's wife, which gave him a feeling of being trapped insofar as he couldn't quit yet knew he shouldn't stay.

But none of this showed as he continued to ride bodyguard on Wardlaw and filled the role of unofficial peacemaker in a town half-tamed, half-wild.

He looked and felt like a man on top of his game until the day a gunman from Nogales came to town.

Coder and Wardlaw were quitting the mine office in mid-afternoon when Wardlaw realized he'd overlooked a document and returned inside.

The gunfighter was relaxed as he rolled and lighted a brown-paper quirley beneath the iron-roofed veranda. He was taking his first draw when a familiar voice caused him to stiffen and instantly drop hand to gunbutt.

Holly was drawing his travel-stained cayuse to a halt upslope beyond the mine's guarded gate.

The gunfighter offered no greeting but simply sat his saddle with both hands resting upon the pommel, youthful features streaked with the grime of long travel.

Coder felt his whole nerve net tighten. Sure, he realized, any Nogales gunfighter was free to show up anyplace anytime, one of the advantages of their freewheeling way of life.

But instinct warned this had nothing to do with chance or coincidence as he went up through the gates to see the receding rider rein in before the Red Wall Saloon. Holly gazed up at the gaudy false-front before dismounting, then with porch loafers watching curiously, he bounced up the steps and shoved the batwings open with both hands like someone who felt he belonged.

For some reason Coder felt like one of his strong black cigars. Right now.

As Deagan's bodyguard, Limehouse felt offended by the effusive way Ace welcomed the gunslinger Holly, after learning exactly who and what he was.

And why shouldn't he feel that way? For over recent times, Limehouse had been the enforcer whom Deagan relied upon to guard himself and his joints, while keeping the Cousin Jacks in line when on his premises, no small feat.

The single blot on the big man's record lingered from the night Coder had cold-cocked him with his gunbutt at the Pontoon Dance Palace. Yet Limehouse had convinced most everybody he'd been ambushed on that occasion and always insisted his get-square with the gunfighter was drawing closer by the day.

It was only when he picked up on the rumor that Holly, the Nogales gunman, had come to settle a score with Coder that he realized he could not risk waiting any longer, and was galvanized into action.

If anybody was going to take Coder down it would be him.

He quit the room like the hero of battles already won.

Foley Wardlaw was staying in that night within his secure circle of Regulators. That left Coder free. Rhea begged him to stay in but the fast gun from Nogales lived by his own agenda. He knew what he needed to do and went ahead and did it.

He headed directly for the nearest saloon, a habit he'd somehow slipped into ever since the death of Toby John. . . .

Later, he realized he'd been careless.

He believed he was fully alert as he mounted the front steps of the Red Wall Saloon to shoulder through the louvered doors, yet subsequent events suggested otherwise.

He barely felt his Colt leaving its holster, it came out so fast and slick.

He whirled lightning fast only to confront Limehouse standing massively before him while a rat-faced saloon bum was flipping his snatched six-shooter away to the man behind the bar.

He'd been careless, the one thing no man of the gun could ever afford to be!

An expectant hush fell as the huge figure came forward to loom before him in the lamplight, fists on hips, radiating hostility.

'Well, well, if it ain't the world-beatin' gunfighter champeen all on his lonesome and with only his God-given mitts to protect himself from big bad Limehouse. Don't you all feel sorry for the wee lad, boys?'

Silently a circle of Red Wall toughs moved to block his way to the door and Coder realized this was a planned set-up. And he'd walked right into it!

The smack of a huge fist into a cupped hand echoed around the Red Wall. Over at the Long Bar, a grinning Ace Deagan raised a glass to the giant and nudged his companions excitedly. Plainly the saloon-keeper was involved.

Limehouse edged nearer, spitting on clenched fists and eyes glittering brightly like the hero of battles already won. By contrast Coder's face remained totally blank as he stood motionless with hands hanging by his sides – while inside emotion was busting loose.

His anger was so fierce he realized it was caused by more than this situation he found himself in.

It was everything that had befallen him since coming to this town.

Firstly, he'd found himself working for a man he despised, and was pitted against poor men he pitied. He then realized he'd fallen in love for the first time in his life, yet with a woman who was not free. Later he'd been forced to beat up on ragged workers, and remained haunted by the ghost of a crazy little man who'd tried to kill him.

And finally now, today, the sudden appearance of a gunslinger who envied and hated him and who might well be his master with the Colts.

What more would any man need to cause him to want either to quit – or strike back?

Without warning Limehouse Jack let loose with a right hook that might well have finished him, had it connected squarely. It didn't, just grazed his forehead but in so doing set something loose in Ryan Coder that couldn't be contained. Every pent-up frustration and uncertainty seemed to release some kind of primitive force inside him as his fist streaked out to crash into a pedulous jaw and grinning mouth like a bomb.

'Aaaahhh!' went the excited mob, but Limehouse appeared merely to falter before retaliating.

And yet this giant was deeply hurt and it showed when his huge legs began trembling and all color drained from his face. Slowly, awkwardly, he raised a mighty right hand only to have Coder smash a right into his face with such ferocity that his huge frame was driven half the width of the room to smash into the wall, then slowly, ponderously toppled forward taking down a sturdy table and three chairs on his way to the floor.

The saloon was hushed.

All eyes were on the fallen giant except Coder's. Some gunman's sixth sense caused him to wheel about to make out the furtive shape of the saloon-keeper in the background . . . the glinting revolver in Ace Deagan's right hand. . . .

He hurled himself to one side and the bullet whistled harmlessly overhead. Voices rose in panic and terror as Coder ducked one way, then went low beneath yet another shot which struck someone in back of him.

Coder snatched a miner's gun from him and touched off a snap shot which sent Ace Deagan crashing into the doorframe with a slug in the shoulder, howling in agony like a hurt animal. And when Coder stretched out a hand to the barkeep for the return of his trusty Colt, it was surrendered to him in meek obedience.

It finished there. And so dominant had Coder been in those moments of red violence that not one man made to block his path as he turned and pushed his way out through the batwings.

Likely nothing had really been solved, he was thinking as he made for the horse. And yet there was no denying he still felt good as he strode on down the street to swing up.

He pointed the black's nose for the mansion on the hill, kicked into a lope and only then realized he'd forgotten about Holly.

He nodded and inhaled a deep breath.

That could wait another day.

CHAPTER 10

THE LAST GUNFIGHT

Sunrise over Chad Valley.

Coder sat up and stretched powerful arms. He blinked and grew aware that he was not alone.

He reached for his Colt .45 before realizing it was the Wardlaws in his room, Rhea lovely and looking drawn yet relieved, Wardlaw pacing the floor with a cigar clamped between powerful teeth. The woman came to him quickly. 'Are you all right? You were sound asleep before we heard about what happened. Were you hurt. . . ?'

He shook his head and swung his boots to the floor, realizing he'd slept fully dressed. Upon reflection he reckoned he must have put in something like a twenty-hour day yesterday. And that was before tangling with two hundred pounds of the strongest

142

fighting man he'd ever faced!

'Limehouse,' he grunted, moving around the cool room flexing suppleness back into aching muscles. The fog was clearing more swiftly now. 'Is he—?'

'Alive but finished, or so Doc says,' Wardlaw supplied with satisfaction. 'Seems like something busted inside him – and we can only hope it's nothing trivial. Anyway, congratulations are very much in order. Deagan's lost his enforcer and—'

'One of them,' Coder countered. 'He's still got Holly.'

He flexed his arms and tilted his head back to loosen the neck muscles. Times like this he was grateful for the fact he was fashioned the sturdy way he was – not a slender and natural-born gunslinger like Holly.

He frowned and reached for the makings, aware of the couple's attention, Wardlaw admiring, Rhea obviously concerned.

'Holly showing up this way so far from Nogales can't be chance or any coincidence,' he said, thinking aloud. 'I saw something in his eye last night that warned me to watch my step.' He shook his head, recalling the enmity the young gun had always held towards him, the envy he'd shown back in Nogales. Offhand, he couldn't think of anybody he'd be less pleased to see here at this time in this still troubled town. . . .

He lit up and arched an eyebrow at Wardlaw.

'What's happening down in the town this morning, have you heard?'

Wardlaw shrugged and looked out the window.
'The Cousin Jacks have gone back to work – something I wasn't sure they would do.' He turned. 'You
know, your whipping Limehouse Jack might have
come just at the right time. I've been anticipating
fresh trouble from my enemies for days . . . felt it in
my bones. Also I'm told that if you'd lost out to
Limehouse, Deagan was ready to whip up the Jacks
into closing me down again in an attempt to force
me to sell up.'

He paused to smile broadly, triumphantly.
'Instead, looking at you now in light of last night, I
know we're even stronger than before. In short,
we're finally back on top.'

Coder thought he might have believed that but for
a man named Holly.

It didn't surprise him to realize the gunman had
linked up with Deagan, which could lead to
anything. In light of this development, it stood to
reason that the miners, though still at work, must
now be waiting to see how the power players would
resolve themselves. For Deagan had always plotted to
take over the mines and might smell a chance to do
so in what was still an obviously fluid situation.

He drew deep on his stogie.

Until Holly showed up Coder had been ready to
accept the miners' return to work as a sign that
Sedalia had settled, and that he was free to quit.

And he'd desperately wanted to go, for unsettling

personal reasons, yet now he could not. Not while danger still threatened ... and she remained here. . . .

He looked across at Rhea now and felt a slow-fading tightness in his chest.

He then closed his mind to anything but hard-edged reality, calmly announced his intentions, then set about finishing his preparation.

He was startled yet strangely touched when Rhea burst into tears and ran from the room when she saw him buckling on his gunrig again. By contrast, Wardlaw seemed both relieved and elated.

'That's the stuff, Ryan boy,' the big man beamed as they saw him off a short time later. 'Show the scum what we're really made of up here and—' He broke off as a dishevelled figure appeared around the corner of the barn. 'Neeley, what the hell – are you drunk again, mister?'

'No sir, Mr Wardlaw, just had to wish brave Mr Coder all the best is all.' He hiccupped. 'You really are mighty brave, Mr Coder – and I'm sure Mrs Wardlaw certainly thinks so too—'

'And just what do you mean by that, mister—?'

Coder broke off, filled leather and was quickly gone. By the time he was halfway to town he'd blanked his mind to everything ... Rhea ... Wardlaw's ruthlessness ... Holly. . . .

He didn't look back as he focused totally upon on the scene below in what he was beginning to think of increasingly as his town.

'You can't fire me, Mr Wardlaw!' Neeley said. 'On account I quit!'

Wardlaw glared. It was hours later and at the end of his working day the mine tycoon had summoned Neeley to his study where harsh words were exchanged concerning the man's drinking and lack of discipline. Yet Wardlaw suddenly began to hold back a little as he realized that setting aside Neeley's drinking and loose tongue, he didn't want to lose a highly skilled and reliable manager over something probably trivial.

'Go sleep it off,' he snapped dismissively.

'Sorry, but I'm quitting,' the man slurred. 'I've seen too much, suffered too much – so now I gotta quit.'

'Seen and suffered? What the hell are you blabbing about now, man?'

Neeley sucked in a huge breath, a timid man searching for some genuine courage.

'I'm talking about Mrs Wardlaw and our gunman, Mr Wardlaw—' He broke off, swaying. He was still very drunk, and needed to be to come up with what he said next. 'You-you see, I fell in love with Mrs Wardlaw but she always treated me like nothing. But that sure isn't the way she is with Coder. She loves him and it's all over her face whenever—'

Wardlaw punched him in the jaw, knocking him down. His face was ashen.

'How dare you!' he snarled. 'And you're not quitting, I'm firing you, Neeley!' he shouted as a servant appeared in the doorway. 'Pack his belongings and kick him off my land, Wilson. Well, don't just stand there, man! Do it!'

Alone, the rich man consoled himself with a double brandy and was able to think soberly on what had been said, and why. In retrospect it seemed he'd been subconsciously aware of a marked change in his wife's manner ever since the gunfighter's arrival. Suddenly it was all too easy to recall the many times he'd caught her studying Coder as she'd once done with him – with that deep and intense expression in her eyes. He swore. 'I've been a fool . . . a damned blind fool. . . .'

Bitterness choked him, for he'd just begun to sense he had at last regained full ascendancy over his life and his town. Now this. A threat to his status and pride that would be intolerable, if true.

And instantly knew he must know the truth – from the only reliable source.

She was at the piano when he walked in and was struck as always by her loveliness.

But no time for softness or subtleties now. This was as serious as things could get.

'Rhea, is there anything between you and Coder?'

Her head jerked up and she stared at him in wide-eyed silence which her husband interpreted as guilt. Conscious of a quick and sickening sensation in his guts, Wardlaw felt anger rise like a dark tide as he gripped the lid of the piano in shaking hands.

'Answer me, damnit!'

'All right, Foley,' she whispered after what seemed an eternity. 'If you want the truth, then yes, I love him. Don't ask me why or how or anything like that, it's just that I find in him something so fine and—'

'Fine? He's a professional butcher – a dirty Nogales gundog who would blast his own mother if—' His voice choked off and he slapped her hard, eyes blazing. 'And you're just a cheap—'

The doors swung open and Coder entered.

'Something wrong?' he said. 'I heard—'

He broke off when he saw Rhea clutching her face. His eyes snapped at Wardlaw.

'She's just come out in her true colors,' Wardlaw said. 'And to think I trusted her, when all along she was waiting to throw herself at the next bum who happened by—'

'Foley, Ryan is innocent, he doesn't even suspect how I feel about him or—'

'Lying bitch!' Wardlaw raged, and struck her again.

Coder's reaction was automatic. He lunged and punched the rich man in the mouth, knocking him to the floor.

'Ahhh . . . a gunfighter's ethics on full display, eh, gunslinger?' Wardlaw gasped. 'Steal a man's wife then turn into the outraged gallant when the cuckold husband objects!' Then, 'Well, you're fired, goddamnit. Get gone right now before I set the crew onto you!'

'You're thinking loco, so I'll just leave until you calm down. But lay one finger on her again—'

'Get out!'

Coder quit the room while a sobbing Rhea Wardlaw retreated to her sitting room, leaving the king of Chad Valley alone to pour himself a treble.

Breathless and shaking with emotion Wardlaw collapsed into the handiest chair, still enraged yet at the moment unable to do anything more than slump like a tormented King Lear, alone, aloof and beyond comfort.

'Strumpet!' he whispered . . . with not a shred of guilt for the brutality he'd imposed on this lovely, fearful woman he was married to. . . .

He firstly dozed, then slipped into deep exhausted sleep. It was a long time before he awoke with the great house all quiet about him, the clock telling him he'd slept over two hours. He drained his glass and was shaking his head to clear it when a total stranger appeared unannounced in the open doorway.

'Mr Wardlaw?'

He was well built with brushed-back fair hair and wore a double gunrig slung low around slim hips. He might have passed as some rich man's son or perhaps a gifted entrepreneur of commerce and trade, but for the eyes. The mining boss had never seen eyes of such an intense, frozen blue . . . eyes that didn't seem to blink as he approached across the deep pile carpet.

149

'Couldn't make anyone hear,' he explained. He halted. 'Name's Holly.'

The name didn't register for the moment. Wardlaw took another sip before both eyes suddenly snapped wide. 'You're that gunshark I've heard about?' He snapped his fingers, 'By God, yes— Holly. That's it, you've got to be him.'

'Keerect. Holly at your service. And from all I hear, you need me, big man.'

By this Wardlaw had regained his full composure. He looked the stranger up and down and was again conscious of the chill that seemed to come off him, the disconcerting intensity of that blue-eyed stare.

'You've got some nerve marching into a man's home unannounced and uninvited,' he felt obliged to say. Yet even as he spoke he ran the man over with an experienced eye, noting the composure and poise mixed in liberally with something genuinely threatening and dangerous.

'All right, it seems my staff are either asleep or simply unaware that total strangers are invading my home,' he said grudgingly. 'So, what the devil brings you here this time of night?'

Holly flipped his hat, caught it and continued before concentrating on his reluctant host.

'After hearing what happened down town I figured I just might find you in need of a troubleshooter, sir.' He smiled showing perfect white teeth. 'Decided I should put in for the job. Might as well tell you right off I'm the finest shootist you're ever going to see. I hear you've got yourself a whole bunch of ornery miners down yonder there who might bust loose and cause you a heap of trouble any old time. Well, bunches don't come too big or mean for yours truly. So – what about it?'

Wardlaw studied him for a long minute's silence. He was comparing this second visitor from Nogales with Ryan Coder, assesssing their possible strengths and weaknesses.

'How do you get along with Coder?' he eventually asked bluntly.

'Hate his guts.'

'How come?'

'I'm better with the guns yet he gets all the glory.'

The mining tycoon prided himself on his ability to assess a man, and something told him this blue-eyed shootist was exactly what he claimed. Fast and fearless, if he were any judge. And the clincher was, he plainly hated Ryan Coder like a rat hates red pepper.

It felt almost as if some benign force had directed this lethal young man here at exactly the time he needed him most.

Wordlessly he reached out and shook hands. Young Holly smiled – almost like an angel.

To go or to stay? Coder was flipping a mental coin to settle that big question when his brooding mood was interrupted by a familiar voice.

'Hear you've been marched, son?'

He turned and looked into Glede Skelley's creased

and honest face. The miners' leader was heavily grimed from digging copper underground. Yet the grin was surely genuine and the gunfighter from Nogales realized that, in the wake of yesterday's events, this was likely the right time for a simple sit-down yarn with someone he'd come to admire and respect.

They talked quietly and intently over the next half-hour at the bar of the Lonely Crow Saloon, during which time Skelley complained about the dangerous conditions prevailing in the Motherlode Mine while the gunfighter in turn unburdened himself concerning recent events upon Wardlaw Hill.

They were on the verge of parting when the sound which all mining communities dread began to drift low and mournful across the rooftops, jolting Skelley to his feet.

'The alarm signal from the mine!' he gasped. 'Something's gone wrong!'

He was right. When they reached the Motherlode a short time later they discovered that half the main chamber had caved in, leaving nine men dead.

By the time they'd organized the citizens into a unit which was at last able to haul the survivors up out of the shafts, a mob of murderously angry Cousin Jacks was already marching upon Wardlaw Hill.

'Rhea!' was Coder's reaction. Then he went running through misting rain to find his horse.

Foley Wardlaw paced to and fro in a fever of uncertainty and impatience along the great gallery of the mansion until Holly eventually came storming into sight from the town below. The gunfighter covered the length of the gravel drive at full gallop then bounced from the saddle to land in a nimble run that carried him to the broad steps.

'It's bad,' he panted. He gestured at the distant scene below where Shotgun Street appeared to seethe with figures in miners' faded denim. 'A cave-in with men dead and the mob heading here! And it's all your fault, so they claim, rich man!'

Wardlaw spun and strode back inside, followed by a straggle of fearful hands. The gunfighter trailed them into the study to watch indifferently as the tycoon poured himself a huge whiskey and gulped it down. Although danger plainly threatened, the gunfighter was a picture of relaxation as he watched Wardlaw bombard Regulators and house staff with instructions to set up the defense.

'So?' he said when they were alone in the huge room again. 'I guess I didn't expect things to get so busy so fast, Wardlaw. Now, where does this leave you and me? What's the plan? Do we run or fight?'

Wardlaw stared dumbly at the younger man for a long moment in total silence, trying to shut out the sound of that mournful alarm siren. Then he snapped out of it and considered the reality. With an angry mob already clear of the town and heading this way, flight had to be his first thought. He'd set up a strong defense but knew there could be no stemming that human tide tonight, no way of drawing the mob's fury.

He must run, bide his time until their rage had burned itself out, then come back to seize the reins of power once again.

Yet he needed time if he was to escape with his treasures, and found himself swinging to study Holly. Even though having had the gunfighter on his payroll but briefly, Holly had impressed him as few men ever had. He trusted the killer, knew what he was made of and was certain he knew how to get the very best out of him.

He strode to a desk, unlocked it and took out a fat alligator-hide wallet which he proffered to the gunslinger. 'Take a look inside.'

Holly opened it, eyes widening when he glimpsed a solid wad of large denomination notes.

'Hold that mob off while my wife and I get the hell away from here, gunman. There's well over a thousand here. If you do the job right there'll be another thousand after we're safely away, and you can join us.'

Holly fingered the money then looked up with a smile. 'For this, I'd take on the goddamn U.S. Army – boss man.'

'Slater and the boys are down at the stables, getting their guns. They'll follow your orders.'

Holly simply nodded, checked his gun and strode out, a dangerous man exuding lethal assurance.

Wardlaw whirled and took the stairs three at a

time, but halted before reaching the upper floor. His wife stood upon the landing staring at him in an odd way, he thought.

'I'm not going with you, Foley. But don't let me hold you up. You'll take all your money, which is all you ever worried about, anyway.'

'Don't be a fool!' he snapped, gesturing in direction of the town. 'They've gone loco. Come on, no time to waste, woman!'

She darted away. He seized her by the arm but she broke free. In doing so she struck a small table sending a lighted kerosene lamp crashing to the floor where it immediately broke and burst into flames. Rhea screamed and drew back but Wardlaw, ignoring the fire, cornered her and seized her by the wrist, his eyes half crazy now. 'I know why you want to stay! It's Coder. But he's not having you now or ever—'

He broke off at the sound of quick steps below and whirled to confront the impossible – Coder charging up the stairs with gun in hand, at the end of a desperate ride that had left the raging miners far behind.

Instantly, the gun in Wardlaw's hand roared and the gunfighter hurled himself violently to one side, unable to shoot for fear of striking the woman. A raging Wardlaw was lining him up in his gunsights again when a small pistol shot rang out behind the man and he stiffened then turned slowly to stare disbelievingly at his wife with the little two-shot in her hand, which he'd given her once for her protection.

He breathed her name once then fell as flames

155

from the upset lamp began raging up the curtains behind him.

There was barely time for Coder to sweep the half-swooning woman in his arms and flee the building, so quickly did that splendid house erupt into fiery chaos all around.

Once clear, he ran and kept running while the sounds of wild cheering arose a mile below, where the mob had halted to stand shaking their fists in triumph as flames leapt ever higher into the night sky – fierce sounds in this night of terror which were soon to be repeated when the word spread that Foley Wardlaw, the miners' enemy, was dead.

Ace Deagan and the gunfighter from Nogales were drinking whiskey together in the gray of early morning in the bar-room of the Red Wall Saloon, when a light footfall sounded.

The expectant look creasing Ace Deagan's features froze when the powerful figure of Ryan Coder filled the doorway. He barely managed to croak, 'You? They said you went up with the house!' before Holly shouldered him violently and went into his deadly lurching draw.

The deep-throated roar of warring .45s filled the room and Coder was falling with Holly's too-fast bullet in him somewhere, crashing down behind a heavy chair. Two snarling shots ripped into the chair before Coder rolled into sight on the opposite side with his big gun spewing shot after murderous shot in response, to buckle the young gun in the middle with his first shot, then sent him reeling blindly backwards with a sudden third eye in his forehead to crash onto his back, never to move again.

In that instant, Coder's smoking cutter had swung to cover the saloon-keeper. But Ace Deagan was never a fighting man, and when the first wary citizen squinted round the doorframe moments later, the sight that met his gaze was the saloon-man down on his knees pleading for mercy from a Ryan Coder who was no longer holding a gun, nor ever would again.

It was over. Yet right across a hushed and shaking town there was suddenly a strange sensation in the very air – that something was about to begin.

Coder was standing in the sunlight on the upper gallery of the Miners' Rest Hotel two hours later when Glede Skelley appeared down below in the street. Yet even had the miners' leader showed up toting a six-gun in either hand and with fifty miners to back him up, Coder would not have raised a finger in his own defense. For in this somber morning he was no longer the fast gun from Nogales but a man changed forever by circumstance, understanding and something even stronger.

But Skelley had come alone and climbed up the stairs to him with a half-grin to gaze out over a dazed yet peaceful townscape. Then he said, 'How is she, Ryan?'

'Resting.' Coder indicated the closed door in back

of him. 'Doc says she's only suffering from shock.' He paused to grimace. 'Like most of this town, I guess.'

'If Doc Doolin says a thing, you can believe it.'

Coder nodded and somehow dredged up a smile. The town appeared drab, gray and smoky below them. Yet there was something tangibly different in the very atmosphere as folks went about their business, each coping in his or her own way with the disaster of the cave-ins, the permanent closure of the mines, the loss of life for both the good and the bad.

The two gazed up at Wardlaw Hill. No proud mansion stood there now, only a blackened ruin against the morning sky as testimony to the night's rage – both mansion and madness just a memory in the cool light of a new morning, and maybe a new beginning.

Coder cleared his throat. 'Guess the mines could be shored up and—'

'Nope,' came the emphatic response. 'We had us a meeting at first light and agreed the mines always proved bad for us – over time. We're planning to pool our resources and go in for ranching. Er, you got any plans, Ryan?'

He did. And excusing himself, Ryan Coder went in to see if she was awake yet and, if so, to ask what she thought of his plans – for the two of them.

For while Rhea had slept under Doc Doolin's sedatives he had finally stopped denying what he knew had begun the instant they'd met. But before he could even admit he'd fallen in love for the first and last time in his life, he'd known she must be free to love him, while he in turn had to be free of the gun forever.

She awoke again at noon and they made their plans. Wardlaw's fortune had been left his wife in his will and they would utilize this to build homes for the impoverished miners and offer them employment on the ranch. Rhea wanted the poor to have good lives and the town to become peaceful and prosperous. By contrast, mostly all Coder wanted now was for her to be safe and happy, and he already had a strong hunch he would be able to ensure that, given time.

For most of all he simply wanted to be with her forever, if it could be that way. . . ?

'Of course we will be both – happy *and* forever,' smiled Rhea, and kissed the ex-gunfighter from Nogales before healing sleep claimed her once more.

He quietly left the room and went looking for Glede Skelley to break the good news.